Secondhand
HORSES

D0204521

© 2013 by Lauraine Snelling & Kathleen Damp Wright

Print ISBN 978-1-61626-569-4

eBook Editions:
Adobe Digital Edition (.epub) 978-1-62416-008-0
Kindle and MobiPocket Edition (.prc) 978-1-62416-007-3

All rights reserved. No part of this publication may be reproduced or transmitted for commercial purposes, except for brief quotations in printed reviews, without written permission of the publisher.

This book is a work of fiction. Names, characters, places, and incidents are either products of the author's imagination or used fictitiously. Any similarity to actual people, organizations, and/or events is purely coincidental.

Cover illustration: Jamey Christoph / lindgrensmith.com

Published by Barbour Publishing, Inc., P.O. Box 719, Uhrichsville, Ohio 44683, www.barbourbooks.com

Our mission is to publish and distribute inspirational products offering exceptional value and biblical encouragement to the masses.

 Member of the
Evangelical Christian
Publishers Association

Printed in the United States of America.
Dickinson Press, Inc., Grand Rapids, MI 49512; February 2013; D10003732

Secondhand HORSES

Lauraine Snelling *and*
Kathleen Damp Wright

the
S.A.V.E.
Squad

BARBOUR
PUBLISHING

Dedication

Kathleen—
to Jane Owen, delightful writer, for the seed of *The Chicago Manual of Style* and even more for our friendship that knows no bounds.

Lauraine—
to my father, Laurel Clauson, who gave me my first pony,
an obstinate Shetland named Polly, when I was five.

Acknowledgments

Many thanks to those who were willing to share great pictures, laughs, and adventures researching this book. Thanks to the horse experts: Kitty, Bonnie, Debbie, Liz, Ellie, and Stuart. The miniature horse people: Becky, Debbie, and Clint. Thanks to Laurie for medical questions; the Jacksons for the right house for the ranch; Facebook friends and fellow adventurers Sue, Ambria, and Brooklyn. Much love to Fred for living with a working writer. ~ Kathleen

Always, always to Jesus for making all of
us different and loving every one of us the best.

Chapter 1

Deep Trouble

Sunneeeee!" her mother called from the house.

"Bounce, bounce, drop, slap, clap! Bounce, bounce, drop, slap, clap!" In rhythm with her chant, eleven-year-old Sunny slapped her bare feet on the trampoline, seat dropped, hit the trampoline deck with her fists, and, while airborne, clapped her hands over her head. "Yayness! Next time, faster!" She pushed off, her breath coming in gasps. "Then—faster—then *faster*—"

Fridays were the *best* because they meant no school for the weekend. And this weekend would not be normal. It would be *rocko-socko* wonderful.

Tomorrow night the S.A.V.E. Squad—Sunny, Aneta, Vee, and Esther—would explore the last night of a traveling carnival in Oakton—*alone*. A first for all four eleven-year-olds. Sunny's Uncle Dave would drive them and had promised to go off and amuse himself. Vee had the Anti-Trouble Phone—the ATP. Afterward they'd stay at Sunny's uncle's ranch—complete with horses—hours of yayness. Could it get any better?

Oh yes. This was a major yayness weekend.

"Dinner!" Her dad *never* called them in for dinner.

Startled by the deep voice, Sunny lost her tucked position, landing on her side with her legs flipping over her head. *Ouch.* Her neck kinked into the deck. Two smaller flopping bounces and Sunny scooted off the padded edge, heart beating wildly. Not because she'd been bouncing, slapping her hands, and pushing off for nearly half an hour.

Because she'd just remembered about dinner.

Pounding in from the side yard and up the back deck steps, she burst through the Dutch door into the large, airy kitchen. Four pairs of eyes turned toward her. Only her youngest brother, seven-year-old Peter, smiled, and his wobbled. Mom, with springy red hair like Sunny's, sat in her regular seat in the ladder-back chair at one end, and tall, skinny Dad at the other end. Her two blond brothers sat side by side with an empty seat across from them.

Deep trouble.

Ugh.

"Hello, Sunny," Dad said calmly, as though his face weren't flushing red like hers did when anger grabbed hold of her. While she slid into her seat, she watched a cord in her father's neck pulse in and out. To her lifetime recollection of getting into trouble, she'd not seen her father's neck do that before. Creepy cool.

"I'm sorry, I'm sorry!" she burst out, grabbing her napkin and spreading it onto her lap.

James—the older of the two boys at nine years old—had his napkin up to his mouth, fake coughing so their father wouldn't see him laugh. Laughing when Dad was mad was not a good idea, and James knew it. Tenderhearted Peter looked ready to cry.

"I'm sorry. I started it. . . ." Sunny's voice trailed off. That's when she smelled it, although it was so pungent she couldn't imagine why she hadn't smelled it out on the tramp. It was icky-strong, the way spaghetti smells when you go out to the tramp just for a minute and get distracted by the rhyme of bounce—seat drop—slap—clap. Pasta burned. Stuck to the pan. As in, not useful for dinner. The huge unopened jar of marinara stood guard on the sink next to the soaking pan.

Dad gestured toward the stove. "Yes, you started it. That's fine. However, finishing is the other half, Sunny Lyn." Dad usually had laugh lines around his mouth and at the corners of his eyes, only this time the lines were set for trouble.

He'd used her middle name.

"I'm hungry," James said, tipping his head toward the fridge and wiggling his eyebrows at his sister.

"Still waiting," her mother said.

Another *ugh*. She'd been so lost in the potential consequences of forgetting to follow through *again*, she'd forgotten that it was still her night to do dinner. She had to fix *something*—a family rule. Leaping to her feet, she sent the chair crashing behind her.

"Sorry! Sorry!" She made a face, picking up the chair to set it back in place. Dad looked at Mom. Mom made her "no, wait" face. Sunny headed for the pantry, grabbed three cans of tuna fish, opened and drained them, then added mayonnaise and sweet pickle relish. She carried a loaf of Mom's homemade bread to the table on a cutting board before racing back for the bowl of tuna fish. After thanking God for their food, James's lip curled—he didn't like tuna fish sandwiches. Everyone sliced off two slices of wheat bread and passed the tuna fish bowl.

"That's it?" James was enjoying this way too much. Sunny narrowed her eyes at him. *Don't push it, bro. I know you're afraid of what's under the bed.*

"James," Mom said. "You won't starve."

While everyone munched on their sandwiches—Dad and Peter made a second one—Peter told Dad stories about what his best buddy had done while they'd been doing science over at his house. She knew he was trying to make Dad use those laugh lines, but while Dad listened and nodded to Peter, his gaze never left Sunny.

She felt lower than the rug on the kitchen floor. Her sandwich tasted like something in a really old bag lunch from a field trip to the Middle Ages; she left most of it on the plate.

After a miserable dinner, the boys and Mom cleaned up while Dad disappeared, cell phone to his ear. Sunny, sent upstairs to her room, gulped back tears. Minutes ticked by. The longer her parents had to think, the worse it would be for her.

All the things she'd left unfinished stomped through her mind. The English composition on friendship. Half done. Math problems half done for two days. A history test on the Middle Ages Monday, and she hadn't finished the activities for it yet. She groaned and threw herself back on the bed, smushing the clean clothes her mom had left that afternoon for her to put away. Who knew what her parents would think of if they remembered all *that*?

She bolted upright.

The carnival.

The sleepover weekend at Uncle Dave's after.

The S.A.V.E. Squad.

Dad and Mom would ground her from *everything*.

During the summer, the four Squaders had been thrown together as Junior Event Planners. Although they hadn't had anything in common but their differences, they'd had one adventure and then another and found that being different didn't mean they couldn't be friends. Sunny liked that. She also liked that the Squad's name was formed from the first letters of each girl's name. She *especially* liked that the letter *S* was first.

Squeezing her eyes shut, she ordered herself to come up with a Great Idea. She had bazillions of Great Ideas. Now she only needed *one*. Right. Now. Of course, the idea to go jump on the tramp while cooking spaghetti hadn't turned out to be so great, but—

"Sunny," Dad called from the bottom of the stairs.

Ugh. Ugh. Ughness.

Sunny descended the stairs, one slow step at a time, thinking in beat to the weight of each foot. *One. Great. Idea. Now.*

Anything to hang on to this weekend.

Moments later, her dad speared her with a look and said in his Consequences Voice, "What would you do if you were me and your mom and had a kid whose forgetfulness impacted other people?"

Mom, Dad, and Sunny were sitting on the floor around the Quinlan Tribe Table, a low, round coffee table where the Quinlans decided "tribe" vacations, how to spend giving and fun money, resolve brother and sister issues, or negotiate consequences. Sunny had been at that table many times for the latter.

Taking a deep breath, Sunny recited the Great Idea that had plopped into her mind on the second-to-bottom step. "I'd send her to her beloved uncle Dave's ranch for two weeks to do school and be a ranch hand and learn to finish fun stuff at the ranch." It came out in a rush. *Hmmm.* She wished she hadn't added the word *fun*. Consequences were *never* supposed to be fun.

She waited for the verdict.

Chapter 2

A Brand-New Sunny Starts NOW!

The largest backpack the Quinlans owned, stuffed with all of Sunny's school materials and a laptop, leaned against a small dresser in the large bedroom. Next to it sat her mom's suitcase. Flinging out her arms, Sunny spun again and again. This Great Idea had worked faster than she could spell *feudalism* backward. Two hours earlier she'd been in Deep Trouble. Now she was a ranch hand at her uncle's ranch. Here she would finish everything—and on time.

For a moment, she stood in front of the open window across from the door. Other Novembers had meant early winter and rain, but not this year. Sunny was still wearing her capris and T-shirt. The weather-beaten wooden rails of the corral that broke up the wide, long meadow behind Uncle Dave's Oregon ranch house looked like a stiff wind would blow them down. She couldn't wait to get started learning how to take care of Shirley and Mondo, her uncle's secondhand horses.

Oh.

And homework catch-up. Of course. She would *dazzle* her parents with how much she would finish here. She gave another quick spin and skipped out of the room. Starting *now.*

"You're the coolest of the rocko-socko uncles on the planet," Sunny said, winding her way through the packing boxes. She finished her skip into the kitchen with a big hug around her much taller uncle's waist. "I'm still in shock my parents went for my Great Idea."

Uncle Dave stood scratching his head. Boxes, stacked to his shoulders, ran across the common entryway and into the living room opposite.

"You never know with parents, Sunny girl." Her uncle returned the hug. "Sometimes they know more than you think they do."

"What do you mean?"

"So many boxes, so little interest." Her uncle had returned his attention to the boxes. After a moment, he blinked and seemed to notice her standing there. "Will you be lonely way out here? We're about as at the end of Oakton as you can get and still be in Oakton."

Sunny shook her head. "I'll be on video chats with Mom for school." She hugged him again and then pulled open a box. "And I'm *sure* you'll let my S.A.V.E. Squad friends visit. A lot."

"Eesh. Surrounded by little girls? That will be strange for this bachelor."

"We're not little. We're eleven!" Sunny huffed. "And it's your fault you're not married."

"Right."

"I'm ready to start finishing things. What do you want me to do first?"

"I think I need you to clean out one of the outbuildings before we can start setting up this house." He rubbed his face. "It's been nearly two months that I've been living out of boxes. Time to settle in. There's probably a lot of junk in those buildings. This old ranch hasn't been cleaned out since the last owner left over five years ago."

Bouncing on her toes, Sunny said, "I'll start right now. You won't be sorry you said yes to me for two weeks!"

He glanced out the kitchen window. "Dark now. Getting late."

"I don't care. I *want* to start now. This is the new Sunny!" As she struggled with the front door, he called over his shoulder. "You've got to lift and pull at the same time." More to himself, he muttered, "The screen door squeaks, too. I have to take a look at that." He flapped a hand at the boxes as if to shoo them away and meandered over to the fridge. "You hungry?"

"No," she said over the screech of the front door. Although dinner had been those disastrous tuna sandwiches, she was too excited to be hungry. Once on the front porch, Sunny twirled around and around, staggering toward the large oval of overgrown grass and weeds in the middle of the circular gravel driveway. The final spin overset her balance, and she tumbled into the oval, panting and snorting. The stars were just beginning to come out.

"Okay, outbuildings. You are about to meet Sunny the Finisher." She jumped up and trotted over to the three buildings. She chuckled. "It's like the three-bears buildings. The barn is Papa Barn, the middle is Mama Shed, and the laaaaassst is the Baby Lean-to!" The largest of the three buildings was a newer barn. Pulling open the door, she stuck her head in. Right inside the door were the stairs on the left to go to the haymow that was loaded with hay. Maybe it was straw. She couldn't tell the difference, but she knew that horses ate one and stood on the other.

After the stairs were three open stalls. On the left of the barn was the tack wall with Shirley and Mondo's saddles, bridles, and all that other stuff that horses needed. Everything looked like a barn should. Trust Uncle Dave to take care of Shirley and Mondo before he unpacked boxes. She liked that.

She shut the door behind her and moseyed on over to the right to scratch the noses of Shirley the palomino and Mondo the red sorrel. "Here's hoping playing with you is one of my chores!"

By the time she'd finished talking with the horses, night had definitely descended. She was nearly to the front porch when she remembered why she had come out in the first place.

"Finishing, Sunny, finishing. It's all about finishing." She made her way to the mama-sized outbuilding. Older, smaller, its roof looked like the builder had skipped over every other board. Was it leaning to one side? She tipped her head. Yup. And sagging, too. The double door to the Mama Shed also had a weak side. She had to lift that side up to remove the iron bar dropped into the two rings that kept the door closed. She stepped in. Darkness enveloped her; her foot slid over the edge of something, snapping her head back. Waving her arms, she went sprawling.

So much for a big start in my new Sunny life.

Chapter 3

Attacking the Shed

In the early light of the next morning, the shed's interior resembled a topographic map her dad had on a recent family hike with its short piles and tall heaps of—what? After Sunny propped the door open with two chunks of cement she'd found nearby, she stood with her arms folded across her chest, legs wide. Sunny the Finisher surveying her project.

Junk. Lots and lots of junk. Barely room to walk. No, make that *no* room unless you pretended it was a minefield and hopped through it. Sunny did just that and then dodged the path back to the doorway. At the door, she saw what had banged up her knee and bloodied the heel of one hand: an old yoke, like she'd seen in her history book, that a farmer would use to harness oxen. Next to it lay two rusted spurs with sharp-looking spikes. She tossed them to the side where they hit the wall and slid down into an old bucket. The bottom of a fan rake tipped over that. Why would someone save a broken rake?

This cleanup just might take until she graduated from middle school, but nobody finished unless they started. She pounced on a broom that had retained enough sweeping bristles to do some good and started sweeping vigorously. Whipping the broom around each obstacle raised clouds of suffocating dust that sent her hacking and choking outside.

Uncle Dave, carrying out a couple of empty boxes to the porch, called over, "You sure you're up to this, Sunny girl?"

"No—*cough*—problem," she gasped, waving confidently. "Just waiting for the dust to die down." Her throat had dried; she had to swallow a few times. "I'll have this finished so fast you won't know what hit you!"

Since the shed showed no signs of giving up its dust storm right away, she set the broom against the door and wandered over to the lean-to. Pretty basic. Three sides, a slanted roof, and an open front. More rusted farm equipment Sunny didn't recognize. She'd definitely made the right choice on cleaning out the tractor shed. This lean-to would involve pushing a whole lot of heavy stuff somewhere else. Something scurried behind the lean-to. Curious, Sunny peeked around the shed, and a happy smile curved her face. At the back of the lean-to, completely hidden from the front, rested an old trampoline. The bed was still on it. She counted the legs. Two looked bent. Still usable. More springs still on it than not, although they were rusty. Everything was rusty around here.

It took her a while to drag out the trampoline and confirm that, yes indeed, this tramp was still usable. While she lay on her stomach on it, propping up her head with her hands, her eyes drooped. The sun was sooooo warm on her shoulders and back. Raising heavy lids, she surveyed her domain. Some wooden boxes, the slatted kind from back in the day, were piled crookedly behind the tractor shed.

The tractor shed. Her eyes flew wide open. She had to finish the tractor shed. The best place for the tramp would have to wait. She rolled off the tramp and hurried to the tractor shed where sunlight caught the remaining dust motes in streams. Almost magical. She sneezed. Now where had she put that broom? Not by the stairs. *Hmmmm.* In the back to the right, stairs leading to who knows where. First ranch hand, house helper, and now explorer. Uncle Dave was the best. When she and the girls woke up tomorrow, she would wear one of her uncle's cowboy hats and take them on a Mystery Tour.

She leaped over the buckets of old bridles and bits, tractor tires, a large coiled rope, a partial bale of old hay, plus bits of unidentified "shed stuff." Up the stairs, she landed lightly on each wooden step. While delightfully creaky, they were solid.

"Wow!" Her head popped up, and she viewed the wide-open space before her. Just ahead, a boarded-up window had cracks of light framing it. Once at the top, she took care to make sure each footstep landed on a floorboard and not in the gaps that filtered dust to the downstairs. "This would be a great S.A.V.E. Squad clubhouse." Making a face, she shook her head. "If we cleaned all this stuff out."

The floor was loaded with "stuff." An old engine machine-y thing stood against the wall. More old tires, parts of calendars, dried-out paint cans with little stuff in them. The previous owner didn't throw out anything. Lots of mouse droppings. Sunny wrinkled her nose and scanned the ceiling. Old birds' nests perched on the beams with white and green drippings. She would definitely have to show the girls *this*. The loft, not the droppings, although the white and green stuff would kill it for Vee as a clubhouse. Vee had this thing about bugs and doo-doo, thanks to her Twin Terror stepbrothers.

A wooden frame with a side hinge signaled a window in the back wall. Sunny made her way to it and inspected the latch. How cool would it be to have a giant's view of the back of the ranch? She jerked the latch. Nothing. She leaned on it and jerked again. A bit of a move then it slid back, and the window slowly began to groan outward with

Sunny clinging to the latch. Half her body hung over the ground that seemed very far below, supported only by the splintery window that groaned louder with each passing second.

Chapter 4

Close Call

"Yiiiikes!" Her left hand fumbled for the window frame. Yes! Relief, when she scrabbled onto the frame, then a big *OW* as the quick prick of splinters followed. Sunny hated splinters, but she would *really* hate falling to her death before the freedom of summer vacation just six short months away.

With a deep breath and holding in her stomach for more backward muscle power, she squinched her eyes shut, told her legs to lock tight, and pulled back. Her foot slipped forward and waggled wildly, trying to get support from the air. Visions of James inheriting her room filled her head; she grunted and pulled back again.

Finally, both feet connected with the edge, then further in, then all of her body back into the loft. With trembling fingers, she let go of the window, collapsing on the dirty floor, sending up poofs of dust and dead flies.

"That was not a Great Idea," she announced after she had convinced herself she truly was alive. A few more deep breaths and then she stood by the window's right side. "But I do want to see what's out there." Pushing the window out and firmly gripping the left side of the frame, Sunny leaned out and looked below. Behind the shed lay more tractor tires and slatted wooden boxes leaning crazily. More stuff to clear out. She shifted her gaze to the tramp, down to the ground, and back to the tramp. She felt her eyes widen.

Since the ceiling was low in this shed, the drop from the loft window to say, a trampoline below, would be about as long as Uncle Dave was tall. Six feet. A rocko-socko complete yayness seat drop. It would be worth tugging the tramp over to below the window.

She had so many Great Ideas, she amazed herself.

After placing the tramp in the absolute perfect position and rubbing her hands in glee at what the Squad would say, Sunny returned to her sweeping. No way could she get the floor clean without moving everything out. She'd put some boxes away inside the house instead; then later, before she and her uncle left to pick up the Squad, she'd move everything.

Her first attempt at finishing dinner was a blazing success and completely blotted out the Stinking Spaghetti of the previous night— at least in Sunny's mind. She made boxed mac and cheese, watching the cooking macaroni like a hawk. She'd eaten the mac and cheese. Finished.

It wasn't *her* fault that Uncle Dave thought boxed mac and cheese should be banned in all fifty states and wouldn't eat it. All in all, with the rocko-socko discovery of the tramp and cooking a homemade meal, it had been a great day. Tonight would only get better.

The S.A.V.E. Squad was heading to the carnival.

Chapter 5

On Their Own

W hat's up, Sunny girl?" Uncle Dave shot her a quick look across the truck as she pointed out the turn to Esther's house and told him how close the girls lived to each other and hadn't known it until the end of the summer.

"Oh, I'm just happy. You saved me from Deep Trouble last night. I get to be at the ranch. Trust me. That dinner disaster consequence could have been a *lot* worse."

"I remember when I was a kid—" Her uncle swung into Esther's driveway. "Oh. Sorry. I know I hated it when adults used to trot out the 'when I was your age' stuff. I'm just glad for the help—especially with that shed."

Umm. That shed. Yes, well. . .she'd get on that first thing in the morning. Nothing would stop her from finishing *tomorrow*.

Esther's mother cupped her hands around her mouth at the open front door. "She'll be out in a minute!"

Turning off the truck, Dave nodded and turned back to Sunny.

Now was a good time to change the subject away from the shed. "So were you going to say how you never got in trouble? That would not be helpful."

Dave threw back his head and laughed the rat-a-tat rifle laugh. It sounded like the blast of many bullets one right after another. She swallowed her chuckles. "Well?"

"No, it wasn't going to be that. Your mom would make sure you knew I was no angel. In fact, Sunny, they used to call me—"

Dark blond Esther ran up to the truck, pulling the edge of her shirt down over her jeans. "Hi, Mr. Martin. Hi, Sunny. Carnival at night! By ourselves, right? Can't wait!" Her hazel eyes were beaming.

Her mother approached the truck to meet Uncle Dave—to make sure he didn't look like a criminal, Esther whispered to Sunny.

At Vee's house, her mother and stepdad, Bill, waved from the front step as black-haired Vee barreled toward them, stuffing folded money into the front pocket of her jeans. She was smiling a smile that only showed up for rocko-socko events. Her almond eyes, so deep brown, sparkled. "Hi, Mr. Martin. Hi, Squaders! Aren't you glad we all live so close? Just one more stop for Aneta. I want to ride the swings."

"I want to do the Death Drop!" Sunny bounced after buckling her seat belt. She turned to the girls in the backseat, who were also buckling themselves in.

"You won't get Aneta on that, for sure," Esther responded seriously. "I think I'll have to keep her company so she doesn't get snatched by someone while you two are on the wild rides."

Trust Esther not to admit *she* didn't want to ride a wild ride.

As the truck turned into Aneta's gated community, Sunny told Uncle Dave the gate code. He punched it in, hit the POUND sign, and the gate swung inward. She saw him take in each large house, many of which had its own pool. "Fancy," was all Uncle Dave said.

"Aneta's mom is a lawyer," Sunny said as they pulled into the driveway. "She is going to give you the third degree when you're driving her daughter anywhere."

"She met me at that barbecue after the Great Cat Caper, remember? Besides, my honest face will automatically convince her." He contorted that face into a monstrous expression at the same moment a cool, professional voice sounded next to his left ear.

"Mr. Martin? You are driving the girls to the carnival and back to your ranch tonight?"

Startled, he turned, his face still twisted. Aneta's mom jumped back, equally surprised. Dave's face fell into the crinkly rat-a-tat laughing face Sunny and her family loved. Aneta's mother's face, on the other hand, transformed into the no-nonsense lawyer face the girls had seen in their very first adventure. Sunny wasn't a criminal, so it didn't scare her. Okay, so maybe it scared her a little. Who she really felt sorry for was Uncle Dave. He had looked like a dope in front of pretty Margo Jasper.

"—and so I'm at Uncle Dave's for two weeks to practice finishing things!" Sunny took a bite out of her hot dog and then inserted a wad of blue cotton candy. Uncle Dave's surprise carnival money was a nice treat. The girls sat at a picnic table just inside the chain-link fence to the carnival.

Aneta nearly choked on her own cotton candy. "Your mouth and lips are *blue*, Sunny. Are mine?"

After swallowing, Sunny nodded, and stuck out her blue tongue.

True to his word, Uncle Dave had paid for their tickets and gotten "lost" as he promised so they wouldn't be treated like little kids. "You won't see me or hear me," he said. "I hear a candy apple calling my name. If you want to watch someone walk off with two armfuls of stuffed animals, come find me. Plus,"—he patted his phone—"I need to talk with people about getting the ranch going. I'm set until it's time to take you to the ranch."

Esther pushed her hair behind her ears. She pulled a wispy strand of pink cotton candy off the puffy mass and laid it on her extended tongue. The girls watched it melt and turn her tongue and lips a neon pink. "If it had been me forgetting things, I would have been grounded for life," she said around the melting pile. It came out sounding like "whee forwetting hings, rounded—*swallow*—for life." She cocked her head at Sunny. "Although usually they ground me from the computer. That's a killer for me." Esther was the computer whiz of the group and figured anything could be found on the Internet.

Leaping to her feet, Sunny fluffed her curly hair until every hair was spinning on its own. "Everybody done? Let's go find fun!" She began to spin until Esther grabbed one arm as it rotated past and held fast. She was short, but she was solid. Sunny stopped.

"Okay!" Esther said as Sunny staggered a bit. Pointing Sunny's arm forward, she said, "That's the direction we go!"

"What's in that direction?" Aneta wanted to know. Of the four of them, she was the one who didn't like diving into adventure. She'd rather have the adventure explained first. If she couldn't have that, she waited until the other three were waiting for her then would smile nervously and join in.

"We'll find your fun!" Vee said, leading the way. "We won't stop until we find it!"

Esther hurried up next to the long-legged Vee. Sunny shook her head and slung an arm around Aneta's shoulders. Those two. Always wanting to be first. Each of them thought they were the smartest S.A.V.E. Squad girl. Sunny knew they were both smarter than she was. Aneta was, too. For a moment, Sunny's delight in the night dimmed. Were they smart because they finished stuff? And if they were, did that mean she was *dumb*?

Chapter 6

Sunny Starts Something

Esther and Vee were waiting at a corner next to a sign pointing right: PETTING ZOO. The two girls danced around the sign, sweeping their arms toward it like game-show girls.

"This is for us!" Vee said.

"Perfect for the S.A.V.E. Squad!" Esther agreed with a happy bounce.

"Petting zoo!" Aneta squealed.

Sunny snapped her fingers and spun. "Let's go!"

A few more steps and they saw the large pen surrounded by little children. Inside waddled a goose that made Esther laugh with his disgust for some things he picked up, bobbled around in his beak, and then spit out.

"Do you see what I see?" Vee was frowning.

"Yeah," Sunny said. "The animals are dirty, and the pen needs new sawdust."

Aneta pointed out a brown-and-white pygmy goat and a small boy nearby. "Look what that boy is doing. He will get bit if he keeps doing that." Nearby, a large reddish pig with floppy ears seemed to snuffle in agreement.

A sandy-haired boy about C.P.'s size—C.P. was a neighbor boy who was always eating and who had helped the girls out before—was jabbing a cotton-candy paper cone at the goat. Whenever the goat went to grab it, the boy would laugh and jerk it away. The goat stamped its foot, rising up on back legs silently, as though shadowboxing with the pest.

"C.P. would never do that." Esther placed her hands on her hips.

Sunny glanced at Vee and Aneta, who nodded and made faces. When Esther planted her hands—or worse—her fists on her hips, you'd better watch out.

A horse, standing in the middle of the enclosure, was a perfect miniature of a horse in Western movies—a dapple gray, a showy silver tone.

"Oh, look, Esther! A miniature horse." Sunny tried to distract her.

The little horse swished its tail and waggled its head to dislodge a pesky fly. Sunny's brows slammed together. That horse should have a flowing full mane and tail. His coat should shine. It would if it were brushed, but the tangled mane and tail held wisps of hay and small clods of dirt. The horse was quietly chewing a mouthful of hay from a meager pile on the ground near a half-empty bucket of gunky water. The horse's gaze flickered over to Sunny, bobbing its head in a friendly way.

It was too late, though, to sidetrack Esther. "Hey, kid!" Esther marched over to the boy. "Don't do that. It's mean."

"Mean!" Aneta echoed. She was right behind Esther, and, as the tallest Squader, towered over the boy. About the only thing that would make Aneta leap in without thinking was someone being mean to animals. That's what made her such a good S.A.V.E. Squader.

"You're not the boss of me!" The boy poked the goat again.

"I'll distract the goat, and the kid will leave." Sunny grabbed an oversized red bandanna tied to a rail on the metal corral. She would flap the bandanna like a matador with his cape. The mini horse raised its head and neighed, the cutest miniature neigh Sunny had ever heard.

"Aww! You're just the cutest." Sunny dropped the red kerchief on the ground as she slipped through the fence to pet the little horse. She stroked the small velvety nose and whispered, "I wish you could live in my backyard. Hey, why not my room?"

Large brown eyes, fringed with heavy eyelashes, looked up at her. The horse ducked its head—in agreement, Sunny was sure—then stamped its foot right on Sunny's.

"Yow!" She yanked her foot out from under the mini's. The horse hopped backward. Teetering on one foot, Sunny collided with the goat who had backed away from the annoying kid. He bumbled into the boy who, by now, had leaned half his body through the middle rail, waving the paper cone. Boy and goat heads connected with a *craaack*.

Sunny winced. *That's going to leave a mark.* Just like her foot. Flapping her arms, still on one foot, she lost her balance and dropped into the dirty sawdust. The goose, disturbed from its food hunt, flapped its wings, rose up, and dive-bombed the nearest part of Sunny—

Her T-shirted stomach.

Chapter 7

Loose Goose

"Ow! Help!" Sunny immediately exchanged that plea for another one: "Knock it off, goose. We're trying to help the goat!" The goose appeared not to care, darting in and out at Sunny. "Help! Vee! Esther! SOMEBODY!"

The pig began snorting. It sounded like, well, like the big ol' pig was *laughing*.

Vee stepped through the rails to shoo away the goose, and as she did, the goose turned its snaky neck and beak toward her. Sunny, whose howls had turned to nervous laughter, saw her friend turn around and dash for the rails, the goose in hot pursuit. Scrambling to her feet, Sunny watched as Vee rolled under the lowest rail. The girl who did not like bugs and other icky stuff was not going to be happy with what had smeared on her back.

The goose followed.

"Oh no!" This was worse. "Loose goose!" she yelled. "Look out— loose goose."

"I don't care!" Vee yelled back, getting up and brushing off her knees and elbows. "That goose is mean!" She reached behind her and peeled her shirt from her back. "WHAT IS WET ON MY SHIRT?"

The bandanna lay crumpled and beaten into the ground by animals and girls. Sunny bit her lip. She was supposed to get that goat away from the kid. If she hadn't gotten distracted, none of this would have happened.

"Hey!" A rough voice at her elbow caused her to jump sideways. A man no taller than herself glared and then gestured to the corral before bending to step between the rails. A very strong smell—a horrible stench—preceded him. "What's going on? Where's the goose?" He glowered at Sunny like she had tucked the fowl into her back pocket. He had three teeth in the front, holes on either side of the three, and a big mole on his nose. A dirty, red-striped, long-sleeved shirt with the sleeves rolled up hung off his skinny shoulders. He spit when he talked.

Gross.

Sunny backed up.

"Um, my friends are running after it." She pointed at the backs of Vee, Esther, and Aneta, who were arranged in a triangle: Vee running backward in front of the goose to halt its forward flapping waddle; Aneta on one side waving her hands to keep it away from the midway rides; and Esther opposite, bending over with her hands out, biding her time to swoop in and grab the thing. Esther was bossy enough to think the goose would be okay with that. The goose was winning. The group disappeared behind a cotton-candy stand.

The creepy carnival guy began mumbling and swung his gaze to the goat, who had calmed down and stood in the middle of the corral chewing something. "Get over here!" he yelled between gritted teeth and took a step forward. The goat stopped chewing and took an equal step away. That seemed to make the creepy carnival guy madder; he lunged for the goat's head, twisting the tiny horns. The goat struggled silently to free himself.

"Hey! Don't do that!" Before she had time to think, Sunny yelled, pushing herself between the goat and the man. For a few body-stink, bad-breath moments, his three teeth—bared in a snarl—met the deadeye stare her brothers received when they took stuff from her room. Then he whirled and spat on the sawdust. "I'm through with these stupid animals. I'll sell 'em all tonight for somebody's dinner." He disappeared into the crowd.

The pig laughed. In a piggling way.

When the miniature horse nosed Sunny from behind, she turned, scratched its nose, and frowned. "We have got to *do* something." Quiet brown eyes blinked. "You need a nicer place to live. That guy is *mean*."

The Squad would figure out what to do. She ducked between the rails, heading in the direction where she'd last seen them chasing the goose. Moments later she found them.

"Guys!" She slid to a stop, breathless. "You won't believe this."

Esther, with a triumphant smile, held the goose who acted as though it had spent its whole life relaxing in the girl's arms. Silly goose. Esther was panting slightly. When she saw Sunny, her happy smile melted into a frown. "Sunny, if you had distracted the goat like you said, none of this would have happened."

When had it become *her* fault? "What? I didn't do anything. I was trying to *help*, for pizza sake. I had the red bandanna and was going to—" *Was going to* didn't mean *finished*.

Ughness.

Vee was shaking her head. "Sometimes, Sunny, your big ideas are—"

"Dumb." Esther wasn't letting this go.

Warmth rushed to Sunny's cheeks. If there was going to be a fight, it was usually between Vee and Esther. Sunny didn't much like being the one in trouble. Especially since The Spaghetti Event.

Trouble again.

She sighed and pushed her hands through her hair then looked at the dusty hands. Now she probably had dirt streaks running through her curls. Could she do anything right?

"Okay, I'm sorry. It seemed like a Great Idea. Kinda fun, like a matador. . ." Her voice trailed off then surged back in full Sunny power. "Forget the bandanna—you won't believe what I heard from that creepy carnival zoo guy."

"Tell us." Aneta's smile made Sunny feel not quite so dumb.

"He's selling the zoo to be eaten!"

"He's *what*?" Esther clutched the goose so tightly it clacked its beak up at her. "You're kidding."

"He can't do that!" Vee's head tipped toward Sunny, her eyes slanted in what Aneta had named the Vee Stare. "You ate too much cotton candy."

"We cannot let him do that," Aneta said. Her usually gentle face looked like she was ready for a fight.

Motioning the others to join her, Sunny spun on her heel and headed back toward the petting zoo. Aneta fell in step next to her.

"She's nuts. It can't be true," Sunny heard Esther mutter to Vee behind her.

"Yeah, Sunny gets excited, but she's never lied." Vee's voice was closer now, at Sunny's side. No Esther yet. Glancing behind, she noted the shorter girl, still carrying the goose, standing next to a popcorn stand. Sunny frowned. The Squaders weren't easy to convince, but they were usually willing to give it a try if it meant saving animals. It wasn't like Esther to give up on the Squad and just stop and eat.

She worked the inside of her bottom lip and stepped up the pace. How long would it take the creepy carnival guy to find a buyer for the zoo?

In the next moment, Esther had zoomed past them, goose jouncing up and down. She flung these words at them: "C'mon! The popcorn guy—told candy apple girl—Glad it's last night. He can't wait to leave—boring Oakton. We've got to save the zoo *now*!"

Vee broke into a jog. Sunny mustered up her muscles and merged into a full gallop. Now the Squad was together. That thought made her smile while she tried to remember to breathe and run. The jingling change in her pocket bounced with each step: Save. The. Zoo. *Save. The. Zoo.*

While the corral was in sight, they still had some ground to cover to reach the animals. She saw the three remaining animals, but where was the creepy guy? Would the creepy carnival guy have a cell phone? What if he already called someone to come and tow off the zoo? What would happen to the big-eyed miniature horse?

The guy must have a cell phone.

Didn't everyone have a cell phone?

I can't wait to turn thirteen and get a cell phone.

Jingle, jingle. How much money did she have in there?

No matter, once she got a cell phone—

"Sunneeee!" Vee's voice cut into her jumbled thinking.

Ooops. Is this what her mother and father were talking about? Easily distracted. Life and death for the zoo and she was running along thinking of when she could get a cell phone. "What?"

"What are we going to do when we get there? What are we going to tell the bad guy?" Aneta was running sideways.

Jingle, jingle went Sunny's pockets again. *Save. The. Zoo.*

"Don't stop running!" Esther yelled. "We've got to stop this guy!"

"Sunneeee!" Aneta's voice dripped panic.

Jingle, jingle.

A Great Idea burst into Sunny's head. *A big, brilliant, BOUFFY idea*. She wanted to spin it was so brilliant.

"We're going to buy a zoo!" Sunny shrieked as she reached the corral, catapulted over the top railing, and landed smack in front of the creepy carnival guy.

Chapter 8

Trouble in a Truck

I can't believe we bought a zoo." Early the next morning, Sunny sat hugging her knees on the bed.

"That's the fastest rescue we've ever done." Esther sat next to Aneta on the inflatable mattress in Sunny's ranch bedroom. "And cheapest."

"Fifty-four dollars and forty cents." Aneta pulled out a plastic bag of hair accessories and began to comb her long blond hair.

"I only had my allowance," Esther said, flushing, then brightened. "But together our money convinced the creepy guy!"

"Something's not right about all this." Vee stretched. She and Sunny had shared the queen bed. "It was too easy."

"Maybe we are getting good at rescues." Aneta braided the right side of her hair into tiny braids while Esther worked on the left side. The plastic bag sat between them.

"Yeah, Vee," Esther agreed.

"I thought it was cool. The guy even said he'd deliver them." Sunny stood on the bed and turned in a wobbly circle, arms held over her head. "I sort of felt bad calling him the creepy carnival guy after a bit."

Aneta nodded. "He wanted to know what kind of building the

zoo would be living in. It was kind of cute that he wanted to make sure the miniature horse kept his raggedy wagon near him at all times."

"Yeah, cute. So why would he sell the zoo?" Vee asked. "After all that?"

The other three shook their heads. The softness of the mattress finally dumped Sunny on Vee, who shoved her off and stood up. "It's just weird." She held up her index finger. "Weirdness number one: four eleven-year-olds bought a *zoo*. Who does that?"

"We did." Esther grinned. "Last night."

Vee swung her head back and forth, holding up her thumb. "Weirdness number two: they're going to live here and, weirdness number three"—she added a finger—"your uncle doesn't *know* it yet, and"—another finger straightened to join the others—"the final weirdness: the guy drops them off *today*."

With barely concealed impatience, the man had written down Sunny's rather long directions to get to Uncle Dave's house and said he'd be there in the morning. When they ran to find Uncle Dave, however, he'd been deep in conversation on his cell phone and never got off!

Sunny caught phrases like "mare delivery" and other horse words, which was pretty exciting. Uncle Dave was getting more secondhand horses. She'd been right that he'd be okay with a secondhand zoo. Pretty soon there would be enough horses for all the girls to ride one. She couldn't wait. "I thought we could make a rocko-socko breakfast and tell him before the guy comes. Uncle Dave loves breakfast."

The girls agreed. After scrambling into clothes and brushing their teeth, they were in the hall outside Sunny's uncle's bedroom ready to thread their way through the boxes when a truck horn sounded outside.

Too early!

"Uh-oh," Aneta said, speeding up.

"Wait, back to the bedroom!" Sunny put her finger to her lips, pivoted, and ran on her toes back the way they'd come.

"Why?" Esther wanted to know, but followed.

When all three of them had joined Sunny, she closed the door.

"What's going on?" Vee asked.

Sunny reminded them about the groaning front door and the squeaky screen. "We'll have to go out the window." She crossed to the window and tugged it up. No screen. It was one of the things on Uncle Dave's "I'll have to take a look at it" list. If, of course, he ever wrote that sort of list down. He wasn't the most organized of people. Vee was a lot better at it.

Each girl sat on the sill and swung her legs over. "Good thing the ground's higher back here," Esther said, the last to swing her shorter legs up and out the window. She pushed off with her hands and landed on the ground.

Sunny reminded them they would be passing her uncle's bedroom window. They dashed toward the front as quietly as shoes on crushed stone could. A beat-up red truck with splotchy rust on the fenders parked in the driveway.

Bang! A single kick vibrated the side of the dilapidated trailer.

"I bet that's the mini," Esther said.

The creepy carnival guy stood at the back of the trailer. Without a word, he undid the latches on both sides and let the ramp fall. *Bang!* Four animal voices responded.

"You scared them," Aneta said, stepping forward.

The animals didn't want help, only *out*. A second after the ramp landed, the goose flew out low with some serious honking attitude. The pygmy goat followed, bouncing, then a scamper of tiny hooves drummed on the wooden ramp. Both were soon by the right corner of the house where the drive led to the back corral and the—now Sunny realized—*nearly endless forest and meadow.*

"Wait!" Four voices yelled, and four girls glared at the carnival guy.

The miniature horse was next, bucking and kicking. It headed the same route as the other escapees. The pig was a little slower, both in coming out and following its zoo mates.

The carnival guy shrugged. "Your problem now. I told you they was trouble." Disappearing into the trailer, he reappeared with the roughly made wagon. "Now, where you gonna keep *this?*" If he was trying a friendly smile, he would have to practice. No matter what questions he had asked about the zoo being safe, he was still creepy. "You gotta keep the two of 'em together. That horse just loves this wagon. Understand?"

Sunny jerked a thumb toward the barn. "Yeah, I *get* it. They'll be in that barn over there."

"C'mon girls," Vee said, taking off. "We've got to catch that zoo!"

Esther and Aneta joined Vee in darting after the stampede. Amazing how fast a pig could run when motivated by its buddies disappearing out of sight.

Great. Now the next worst thing would be Uncle Dave seeing the zoo before Sunny had a chance to explain. And get them washed. The quick parade of animals had shown they were even dirtier than last night.

The dust from the beat-up red truck's departure settled back onto the driveway while Sunny bounced up and down on her toes, thinking. Good thing Mom always said that her brother could sleep through a tornado. One had just swept through as a runaway zoo. It would be so fun to play with them, she thought, this new idea causing a little spin just thinking about it. If they were going to get them adopted, they would have to make them not grumpy by showing them kindness.

"The S.A.V.E. Squad shall un-grump them!" She cracked herself up sometimes. Over her hilarity, she heard a pig snort to the left of the house. The problem again descended: Uncle Dave did not yet know he had a secondhand zoo.

What to do?

She first heard the groan, then the squeak, then Uncle Dave appeared, squinting on the front porch. Mom said Uncle Dave was the absolute last man to own animals, since getting up at dawn was his least favorite thing to do.

Sunny no longer wanted to spin. Okay, now what? Another pig grunt then a small bleat that sounded like "Baaahhhhhb." Goats didn't talk. Did they?

"Did I hear a truck horn?" He rubbed both fists back and forth on his head. Despite the crisis, Sunny had to giggle. He wore his blond hair longer than Dad, and one side had a big poof of hair. The other flopped right back to flat after each knuckle rub.

"A—a truck?" She widened her eyes and turned in a big, slow circle, shading her eyes as though searching. "Mom says you walked in your sleep when you were a kid, Uncle Dave."

Hooonnkkk!

Sunny stood motionless, her back to her uncle. She had to do something. If the girls *hadn't* gathered up the zoo, those goofy animals would scatter again, every which way, right in front of Uncle Dave. If the girls *had* the zoo under control—sort of—they'd herd that zoo right in front of Uncle Dave. Either way, if Sunny did not warn them, Uncle Dave was going to wake up faster than if she'd poured ice water on him. Now, while Sunny did not have a Great Idea, she *did* know the zoo parading in front of Uncle Dave right after he woke up was *not* any sort of a good idea.

Finishing the turn to face her uncle, she froze. On the left, pushing through the evergreen bushes, was a dirty snout and Vee tapping the pig's back with a stick. To Vee's left marched Esther, the goose under one arm on one hip, her fist perched on the other hip. Uh-oh. To Esther's left, Aneta held the rope leads of the goat and the mini. Even from many feet away in the driveway, Sunny saw Aneta was dirty and the closest thing to a glare she'd ever seen on the usually tranquil blue-eyed girl's face. And Aneta was limping.

Turning back to her uncle, she asked, "Are you awake?" She stepped to his left and took his arm with her right arm. With her left arm, she smacked desperately at the air, hoping the girls would read that as "go away, not now!" More than that, she hoped Esther wouldn't decipher her arm and decide anyway to introduce the zoo to Uncle Dave because Esther thought it was the right thing to do. *Trust me, Esther. . . .* Sunny shot her a silent message and a quick *AHHHHH!* face as Uncle Dave yawned. *It is not a good idea.*

"I hope not," he said inside a second yawn. "Did you feed and water Shirley and Mondo yet?"

Ughness.

She'd forgotten her regular ranch chores with the horn blast that announced the arrival of the zoo. *Sunnneeee!* she yelled at herself. How would Uncle Dave say yes to the zoo when Sunny hadn't followed through with the regular stuff? *Ugh. Ugh. Ugh. Ugh.*

Darting around to his right side so he wouldn't look at her and see the zoo still hovering by the corner of the house, Sunny ran through possible ideas. She could pretend to have a choking fit and make Uncle Dave help her into the house. She tried an experimental cough. No, that wasn't good. Then her uncle would want to know if he should call her mother to come get her. There'd be no escape from the house to tell the girls what to do.

She shot a glance toward the girls. Esther was frowning. Vee was glaring, and Aneta was close. Since English was Aneta's second language, Sunny figured that the "Sunny-arm speak" was probably something she didn't understand. At least they had stopped moving forward.

"I'm on it, Uncle Dave. And then I'll come in, and us girls will make breakfast for you. So go back inside and sleep a little more, okay?"

"Servants," he muttered, following her obediently and yawning again. "I like the idea of servants. There's eggs, bacon, and, um, stuff in the fridge."

"Right. You just leave everything to us." She had him in the front door in another second and pulled the door closed. A whoosh of breath escaped.

That was too close.

Leaping off the porch, she flung her hands high and sprinted to the side of the house.

"I don't like this," Esther said, shaking her head. The goose grumbled.

Vee agreed. "I don't think the pig does either." She gestured to the dust that coated her legs up to her knees. "He didn't want to come back. He was at work rooting up an old garden like he was hired to do it." She brushed at her capris. "Now I look like *I* did the digging."

Behind her, Sunny heard the door begin its early groaning. "What? He's coming back *out?*" She turned back to her friends and began to wave them backward. The mini bobbed his head and jerked the rope through Aneta's fingers. She cried out and dropped the rope. Bending over to regain it with her other hand, she held the reddened palm up. "Sunny!"

41

"Okay, okay, just *don't come out here*. First, we have to wash them and make them look pretty. First impressions are important. Dad says that all the time."

The goat and the mini, apparently thinking they'd been standing still long enough, stepped forward. Aneta dug her sandals in, but the two of them just kept walking, dragging Aneta as though she were water-skiing on dirt.

"Sunny! I cannot stop them when they do that. I already fell once and got dragged." A long green scrape ran from her bare anklebone to halfway up her calf.

Another door groan. Why was he coming out *again*?

Her gaze darted to the front of the house and then took in the outbuildings. That building with all the farm tools and the tractor. The one—she gulped—the one Uncle Dave had asked her to clean out and organize yesterday. *Ugh*. She'd forgotten. She waved toward the buildings.

"The outbuilding in the middle. Put them in there. Once I'm sure it's safe, we'll wash them in the barn. Go!"

Esther and the goose turned to go. "I'm not happy," the shorter girl said over her shoulder. "We need an emergency meeting of the Squad."

"That's for sure." Vee stepped in front of the pig. It backed up. Taking a step to the side, she again moved into the pig, tapping it with the branch, and finally got it turned around, Vee and the pig grunting all the way.

"The goat and the horse are cute when they are not making me ski on dirt, Sunny," Aneta said. Putting a lead rope in each hand, she turned and walked back the way they'd come. The mini and the goat followed.

"I'm coming, Uncle Dave," Sunny hollered, jogging back to the door. She put her mouth to the door where she could hear her uncle tugging. "You have to kinda lift it up." She heaved up on the door handle. "While you SHOVE—" Her own shove carried her right into the entryway where. . .she tripped and fell on the body of her uncle. "Oh, Uncle Dave, are you okay?" Peering down at his face, she parted his long bangs. A large red spot showed on his forehead.

"I—," he said, wheezing, and then gestured for her to get off him.

"Oh." Sunny rolled off and reached to help him get to his feet. He pushed her away and rose, groaning. His hand flew to his forehead.

"Ow." He pressed his lips together. "Ow." Then he slowly turned and headed down the hall to his room. At the doorway, he stopped, turned, and regarded her, his hand still cupped over the red spot.

Sunny was pretty sure that was going to turn into a big lump—a real *goose egg*. Maybe someday he would laugh at getting his own goose egg the day a goose arrived?

"I am going back to bed. I *do not* want breakfast."

She heard his final mutter. "*Servants.*"

Chapter 9

Great Idea or Deep Trouble?

Eager to get to the tractor shed where the S.A.V.E. Squad waited with the zoo, Sunny raced through the feeding and watering of the two horses. Mondo ignored her since he only liked Uncle Dave. Shirley, a palomino with a beautiful white mane and tail, nuzzled Sunny and wuffled into her ear. "You guys have new friends. Wait till you meet them." Then she was off to the middle outbuilding.

The morning light had yet to skip through the wide spaces in the old wooden roof as she slipped through the double doors. The pig grunted. The goose honked. The mini stomped its foot. The goat said, "Baaaaaahb!"

Achoo—dust alert!

"Whoa!" Sunny stopped just inside and peered at the rest of the S.A.V.E. Squad. "Did that goat say—"

With a choking laugh, Aneta responded, "Bob. He says Bob."

Sunny pointed to the goat. "He never said a word at the carnival."

"Maybe he didn't like talking to the creepy carnival guy." Aneta shrugged.

"The pen in here was too disgusting to put them in." Esther

wrinkled her face. "I wouldn't put someone I *didn't* like in there."

Sunny stuck out a foot to prevent the goose from escaping while she closed the doors.

"Hey!" Vee said. "Instant dark!"

"Close your eyes tight, count to ten, and then open them," Esther's voice ordered through the gloom.

Ten seconds later, Vee's surprised voice said, "Hey again! Now I can see. Sort of."

"I found it on the Internet once," Esther said. "There's a water spigot out that back little doorway and a ramp down to it." She leaned against the pen railing. "Since I don't see you with towels and soap, I guess we're just hosing them off?"

Guilt picked away at Sunny. Esther was right, of course, about needing towels and whatever you washed animals with. Sunny's only thought had been how cool it would be to clean up the zoo and parade them before Uncle Dave. She'd forgotten to follow through. Again.

Ughness.

"You're better at this, Vee." Sunny cocked her head at her taller friend. "I forget everything. Everyone says so."

"But you cannot do that anymore now," Aneta said from her place on a very old, very broken saddle on the floor. "You have a zoo."

"*We* have a zoo," Sunny reminded her. The little goat had its feet tucked up underneath him and was settled in next to Aneta. *I wonder what Aneta's mom and Wink the basset puppy would think about a goat?* Aneta might find going home without the goat a little tough.

Sunny moved toward the back door and nearly tripped again over something. Nobody could walk through the shed unharmed. Even the animals were colliding with various broken and rusty bits of forgotten old stuff.

The mini picked his way through some old tires and stuck his nose near her face, looking like he was asking, "What's next?" She grinned and scratch-scratched the white blaze on his silver face. Uncle Dave thought this building had been cleaned out yesterday. She'd have to do it right after they cleaned up the zoo and presented them to her uncle and before the Squad got picked up. She peered in the gloom.

Picked up. *Yikes!*

She gave a little hop and scraped her ankle on a metal bucket. "You guys! We have to hurry! Aneta's mom is coming to pick us all up for church. What *time* is it?"

Aneta checked her watch. "My mom is coming in forty-five minutes. Is that enough to clean a zoo?"

It was. Vee found empty burlap bags and two empty cloth feed bags that they used to rub down the animals. The goose liked the pump, or he just liked anything that Esther wanted him to do. The goat, not so much. Aneta was wet at the first refusal. But between gales of laughter and water everywhere, the zoo was soon rid of all its carnival and escape dirt.

Sunny couldn't wait to get a curry brush on the dapple gray mini. The long, flowing mane and tail would look like white-silver dust when she was through. Maybe moondust. Whatever, it would look better than carnival dust. The horse—all of the zoo—seemed a lot friendlier than when they lived at the carnival. "Okay, guys, we've done it. Now we can show Uncle Dave that rescuing a petting zoo will be okay."

"What are their names?" Aneta asked, stroking the pygmy goat that butted her hand like a dog when she stopped. "His name is Bob, don't you think?"

A chorus of laughter greeted that.

"I already named the pig," Vee said offhand. "Seems like Piggles the Pig to me."

"Great." Sunny nodded in agreement. "Esther?"

"When the goose waddles, his behind goes which way and that. So his name should be Which Way."

"I like it!" Aneta chuckled.

The three girls looked at the mini standing close to Sunny, blowing on her neck. She hunched her shoulders and shivered. It was a crazy cool feeling.

"Snuffy?" Sunny ventured. The small horse turned its back on the girls. "Guess not. I don't know yet. Just not Mini. That sounds like Minnie Mouse."

With the zoo cleaner than before and the pen just as dirty, the girls decided to leave them loose in the tractor shed while they told Uncle Dave how lucky he was to have a secondhand zoo on his secondhand ranch. They headed toward the door, taking care not to trip on all the lurking objects waiting to send them tumbling. First thing tomorrow, Sunny vowed, she'd dive into this mess and make it look amazing.

With her hand on the latch, Vee shook her head. "Like I said before, this rescue was too easy. I mean, we had a couple of scares this morning, but. . ." Her voice trailed off.

"Why can't it just get easier as we go?" Esther asked.

They were halfway through the door when Sunny remembered the trampoline. Grabbing Aneta's wrist, Sunny checked the time. "Oh, yayness! We have time. I want to show you something completely fun-dee-niably wonderful!" She turned and pointed to the stairs that went up into the loft. "C'mon." She hopped over the obstacles.

"Are those stairs safe?" Esther wanted to know, standing at the bottom.

"Yup. See?" She bounded onto each step. "No problem."

"What about talking to your Uncle Dave?" Vee was right behind Sunny. "We still have to introduce the zoo before Aneta's mom comes."

"It'll only take a second, and then you'll see how splendiferous it is and how much fun we'll have whenever you guys come to the ranch." Sunny stepped up into the loft, gave the unlatched window a hearty shove, taking care to hold on to the side of the opening. It swung out with a baby squeak compared to the front-door screen. Cool air filtered in.

When all four stood together, Sunny cried, "See ya!" and jumped out the window.

As her hair streamed up behind her, Sunny grinned. Hearing the screams of her friends above her put this trampoline jump right into the Top Five Great Ideas she'd ever had. It had been worth tugging that old tramp under the window yesterday.

A breath later, she hit the tramp. Three of the rusty legs collapsed on one side. Up in some serious air, Sunny looked down and saw her new landing position was now a slanting *launch pad*. Right into that pile of old wood-slat boxes she'd looked down on yesterday, the kind she'd seen in history books when people shipped stuff.

Bounce!

"Yikes!" Her feet hit first, and landing off balance, her hip and shoulder followed. Her head was still on the tramp when the rest of her body rose like a missile and torpedoed into the boxes.

Crash!

Ugh. Ugh. Ugh.

Instant splinter-fest.

Not daring to move lest more splinters attack her, she rolled her gaze around the boxes on top of her and on each side. This was going to hurt big-time.

The girls' screams were louder now. Sunny could hear each of them as she lay. Her plan had dropped from the Top Five Great Ideas to that other list her parents called You Should Have Known Better.

"Sunneeeeee!" She heard Aneta's wail and Vee and Esther shouting at each other as footsteps pounded down the stairs. "Do not move! Are you hurt?"

Then she heard her uncle's deep bellow and his boots grating on the gravel. "What's going on? Sunny? Girls? Where are you?"

Aneta's voice: "Sunny's uncle! Sunny's uncle! Help!" Sunny bet Aneta had clean forgot Uncle Dave's name and most of her English in her terror.

This was going to *ugh* pretty fast. Sunny swung her legs to the side and then on to all fours. *Ohhhhhhhh. . .*her insides. After a moment the dizziness passed, and she stood. She heard the girls yelling at Uncle Dave and him bellowing at them as he neared the shed.

The shed!

The zoo!

Deep Trouble!

She had to get to him before he opened those doors. Visions of escaping animals *one more time* tore across her mind. She staggered to her feet.

She rounded the corner in time to see the last bit of her uncle's jeans enter the shed.

"Uh-oh." Sunny dashed the last yards.

First her uncle's yell, "What's this—*ahhh*!" Then a piercing, every-sound-at-once noise of the goose, the pig, the goat, and the mini reacting to their abrupt introduction to Uncle Dave.

As she charged through the door, the goat rose on its hind legs, plunging its head up and down as though ready for a charge. Uncle Dave leaped back and tripped on the old coffee can of bolts and nails and stuff. His arms windmilled.

"Sunny!" As his right foot slid over the top of the old wooden yoke with its shreds of leather and caught, his voice pitched higher.

"What have you—" A sickening *pop* sounded a second before a horrible yell exploded from her uncle.

Esther, Vee, and Aneta stood at the bottom of the steps, eyes big, mouths open, clutching each other.

Chapter 10

No More Great Ideas

With the muted voices of the surgical floor waiting room in the background, Sunny inspected her feet. Anything was better than thinking about what had happened to Uncle Dave. One shoelace had bigger loops in it than the other. Mud from Uncle Dave's ranch had mushed up over the toe of the right sneaker. The holes for both sneakers' laces were just slightly off from being exactly across from each other.

This is the worst day of my life. I'll never have another Great Idea as long as I live.

"Code blue, code blue, to room 213," the voice on the speaker urged.

Sunny sat across from her parents. She didn't deserve to be part of the family. The boys were home with a neighbor. At least her parents could have them for kids.

Daring to peek up, she scanned her parents. Dad held Mom's hand while she chewed the inside of her cheek—a sure sign she was stressed. Dad was tapping his first two fingers on the arm of the really uncomfortable chairs. What had happened wouldn't stop playing like a scary movie in Sunny's head.

Aneta's mom had arrived to pick up the girls moments after Uncle Dave fell. She had stuffed the girls into the SUV along with Uncle Dave and zoomed to the emergency room. He'd been hustled up to surgery. The family had made its way through the maze of halls to the waiting room.

It's been over three hours. An ankle wasn't very big; what could they be *doing* to it?

Sunny squirmed when her father's gaze met hers. With Dad, Sunny could expect a wink and a smile just because their gazes met. Not now. There was something in his eyes that Sunny couldn't read.

"Dad, I'm so sorry," she said for about the zillionth time. She'd been saying it since Aneta's mom pulled into the driveway to be met by four screaming girls. Being a lawyer must mean you know how to deal with truly *ugh* stuff because Aneta's mom understood the story while running for the shed. She'd never freaked out once.

Swallowing past the growing lump in her throat, Sunny remembered seeing her uncle laying in a weird way on the floor, his ankle trapped in the yoke. For as long as she lived—and that might not be too long—she would not forget his gasping, and the groans that burst from him as Aneta's mom got him up and half carried him to the SUV. Aneta whispered on the way that her mom worked out. Good thing.

"So you've said." Dad shook his head. "Oh, Sunny."

Mom squeezed his hand, crossed the room, and sat down next to her. The tears that had been sprinkling out on Sunny's cheeks gave way to deep, shoulder-rattling sobs. Leaning forward, she buried her face in her hands, feeling the wet of the tears and snot.

"Honey," Mom said, her left hand rubbing Sunny's back. "Talk to me."

"If I hadn't thought it was such a great idea—" Where to start?

The Great Idea of pulling the tramp under the window instead of cleaning out the tractor shed like Uncle Dave asked? Or persuading the girls to see her Great Idea of the window jump because it was "just for a second"? Or the Great Idea of jumping out the window that made the Squad wail and Uncle Dave wonder what was going on so he came running out and. . .

She shook her head. Her mother handed her a tissue, and she blew her nose. Hard. "If I hadn't had *any* Great Ideas, none of this would have happened. I'm never having a Great Idea again."

"Sure you will, honey."

The doctor, who had explained to Mom and Dad what type of surgery they would be doing on Uncle Dave, appeared in the doorway. "He's in recovery now. Everything went well."

A big sigh whooshed from Mom.

"He'll need somebody to help him get around for a couple of weeks." The doctor looked at Mom. "As I recall, you said he isn't married?"

Like a lightning bolt zapping down and zinging her, Sunny knew what she *had* to do.

Chapter 11

A New Sunny Coming Right Up!

"Uncle Dave was el-supremo before. Now he is the complete yayness of an uncle." Sunny bounced in the passenger side of the minivan as it turned into the ranch.

Her mother glanced at her, shaking her head. "I'm not sure he didn't hurt his head in that fall." At Sunny's look of alarm, she smiled. "I'm joking. It's just—well, I'm wondering if being Dave's nurse, handling the zoo, and the two other horses isn't too big a job for you. Might be easier to start with something smaller." She reached over and squeezed her daughter's knee. "Like, maybe finishing your school-work consistently?"

Sunny chewed the inside of her bottom lip. "I'm going to be the best nurse *and* ranch hand that's ever been. You'll see. We'll do video chats. You can ask me, and my homework will be done!" After a sleepless night of sitting by the window, she had decided to get serious about becoming Sunny the Finisher. New Idea, *not* a Great Idea: she'd practice by being like each of the S.A.V.E. Squad. First: Aneta, the kindest and nicest of the Squad.

Her mom parked the van. Sunny leaped out and slid the side door open. "I still don't see why you got so much microwave stuff. I do all right on my night to cook." *Memory: burned spaghetti. Memory: Uncle Dave hates boxed mac and cheese.* "Oh."

"Let's just say I know sometimes it's nice not to have to cook," Mom said with a wink.

She was *the best*.

The front door screeched open, and three bodies hurtled out. "Sunny! Sunny!"

In the two days since she'd seen them, their grins had returned.

Before the girls descended on the minivan, Mom said quietly to Sunny, "I think you better not mention the zoo until Dave is off the pain meds. Just take care of them and don't let them bother him. I mean it, Sunny."

No problem, Mom. I am now a nice, helpful person who finishes things. Sunny stepped out of the van. "You guys!" A happy spin elevated the bags in either hand. "The Squad!"

Her mother passed them, both arms laden with cloth tote bags. "Yes, I thought you might need reinforcements after school and on weekends. The doctor said Dave's going to need help for about two weeks."

Vee stepped forward and took one of Sunny's bags. "That means two weekends of sleepovers and every day after school."

"Yeah," Esther chimed in. "We get to be part-time ranch hands!"

Aneta took Sunny's other bag. "My mom and Gram say this is a learning and giving opportunity."

The four girls laughed. They knew how Aneta felt about "opportunity." It often meant she ended up doing something way out of normal. But this time it wouldn't be. Not with *all* of them helping with the animals and Uncle Dave. Piece of cake. Especially if she was a great Aneta-type person who finished things.

In the kitchen, the girls and Sunny's mom put away the groceries and frozen food.

"You said you were going to cook for your uncle," Esther said, sliding box after box into the freezer. "I thought you meant, like, *real* cooking."

"I am," Sunny defended herself. "I'm going to make amazing breakfasts for Uncle Dave." That part wouldn't be like Aneta. Cooking and Aneta? Not such a good mix, the Squad and others had discovered. Think *smoke*.

"Good," came a wobbly voice from the small living room immediately across from the big kitchen. "I like a–mm–m–mazing br–r–reakfasts."

The girls trooped into the room. There on the couch amid a bunch of pillows lay Uncle Dave. Sunny explained to the girls in a low voice that he had pins put in his ankle and that was a fiberglass cast around his lower leg. This was a perfect opportunity to practice niceness.

"Here we are," Sunny announced, introducing her friends. Uncle Dave's eyes looked kind of funny, like he was looking at her but not really *seeing* her. He waved a floppy hello. Pillows were supposed to make you feel like you're lying on a cloud, but Uncle Dave acted more like they were stone pillows. One in particular seemed to be sticking his neck out funny. Great! Time to be kind. Sunny darted forward and with a quick tug moved the pillow to the left. Uncle Dave's head rolled with it. "We're here to help you, Uncle Dave."

"Ow," he said faintly.

"Oops." Sunny shoved the pillow back, poking him in the eye with the corner of it. He had to peer at them out of one eye.

"Right," he said, his words slippery and slurred. "I h–hh–ope I surrrvive it."

Everyone always smiled when *Aneta* did things like that. As long as she wasn't cooking, she did a great job being nice and helping. It wasn't going to work for Sunny to be like Aneta. Uncle Dave wouldn't live through it.

Sunny's mom left after many directions. Vee wrote them all down. Sunny's mom raved about how organized Vee was. That decided it. Sunny's next try on finishing: be like Vee for a few days and write down everything to do.

After his eyes fluttered closed, the girls left Uncle Dave to rest and sat around the long kitchen table surrounded by packing boxes.

"Oh, Sunny—Nadine said she's missing you at the library." Esther slouched in a kitchen chair.

"She says she needs one of your Great Ideas," Aneta added.

Vee gazed around the room piled high with boxes. "Man, for a guy who's not married, he has a lot of stuff."

Sunny shook her head. "I don't have Great Ideas anymore. They get me in Deep Trouble. So I'm going to be a finishing kind of kid. Like you guys." She tucked away the thought, however, that it was fun to have Nadine think she used to have Great Ideas.

They moved on to what Uncle Dave needed help with. Vee, being Vee, pulled out her notebook and tiny pen to add to the directions for taking care of Uncle Dave.

"Wait," Sunny said, holding out her hand for the notebook. "I want to make the list so I can finish things."

Vee's eyebrows hit her hairline; she slowly passed the notebook and pen to Sunny.

"You finish stuff. I want to be like you. Being like Aneta wasn't good for Uncle Dave."

Vee smiled. Aneta looked puzzled.

"You're very nice. I wanted to try following through with being nice to Uncle Dave," Sunny explained.

The light dawned in Aneta's eyes. "Oh, and you were like me with cooking instead."

"Right."

Aneta nodded with a hint of a grin.

After a few minutes of Sunny contorting her face to remember what Uncle Dave had told her about the horses and what she remembered doing, she threw down the pen. "I must think harder!" She rubbed her head like her uncle did in the morning, her hair exploding in a floaty frizz. "Ahhhh!"

Aneta, Vee, and Esther tee-heed at the hairdo then plucked apples from the bowl Sunny's mom had left on the table. Esther, sitting next to Sunny, leaned over to see the lists. Sunny covered them. "Not yet. I'm still working on them."

"We could all make our own lists, you know," Esther said.

"Oh, let Sunny do it. She's not hurting anything," Vee said, a stubborn light sneaking into her eyes.

Esther had that ready-for-battle look on her face. Now she was opening her mouth.

Sunny leaped from her seat, throwing her arms in the air. "Okay, guys, we can't argue this time. Really. I mean it. I have to show Uncle Dave and my parents that I can actually finish something, so if you two are arguing, I know I'll get distracted."

Vee glared up at her. The Vee Stare full force. "I wasn't arguing. I was giving my opinion."

"Well." Sunny felt deflated. She lowered herself back into the seat. "You get what I mean."

Esther took a bite of apple and winced. "These are sour." Suddenly she giggled. "Sunny, I promise I won't be sour like this apple. I'll crunch along with everyone else and help you finish stuff."

Throwing an arm around Esther, Sunny surveyed the girls. She loved the Squad. She really did. Who else would give up free time after school and for two weekends to work hard? She frowned. Hmmm. Unless they didn't know how hard they were going to work.

She finished the list a few minutes later and showed it to the girls. Vee said it was a great list.

"On to make dinner!" Sunny announced, springing up from the chair.

Dinner was hot dogs cooked in a frying pan on the stove with not-toasted buns. Although Sunny's mom always toasted the buns under the broiler, the girls had agreed that it might not be a good idea to use a strange oven on night one. A microwave pan of macaroni and cheese—much more fancy than box-style—rounded out the meal. Sunny took in a plate on a tray for the sleeping Uncle Dave to have whenever he awoke.

"After the creepy carnival guy left, the zoo got friendly," Aneta said after dinner, picking up their empty plates and heading toward the sink. "So now we do not have to un-grump them like Sunny said." Vee joined her and together they rinsed the dishes and silverware and placed them in the dishwasher.

"And we were washing them, too. Other than Which Way, they might not have liked it, but they weren't grumpy about it," Vee said.

"Like I said, this has been the easiest rescue ever. Now we need to see what each animal is good at so we can tell people." Esther set her fork down and pushed her not-quite-empty plate away. "That might help them find homes. After homework."

The girls started on their homework at the big pine table as they had promised parents. Every time Sunny started to daydream, she'd receive a little kick on the left foot. Vee sat on her left. If she stared at her paper and book too long, a nudge from Esther jabbed her in the ribs. She wished the girls were staying every day; it sure made school faster. She didn't mean to disappear into her head; it just kinda happened, so it helped to have reminder friends.

Soon after the last book snapped closed, Esther's dad picked up the girls and Sunny was alone. She checked on Uncle Dave. He looked like he was going to sleep all night on the couch. Mom said he might for the first few nights and to let him. She took the tray back. Maybe a forkful or two of mac and cheese. The hot dog was untouched. Poor Uncle Dave.

"You and the ranch are going to be just fine. I'm so sorry I made you fall and break your ankle. You'll see. *I'll finish everything*," she said, even though she knew he was dead asleep.

When she began yawning, it was time to put the zoo to bed. On her way to the barn, she saw the mini standing at the rails as though waiting just for her. And the goose perched on the little horse's back! Funny.

"You looking for a free ride, Which Way?"

The tiny brown-and-white goat standing in the barn opening bleated softly. Which Way flapped off the mini and ducked under the lowest rail to follow her. As Sunny walked past the paddock into the barn, she noted the pig had already put himself to bed, wide side heaving up and down with each snuffly snore. One of his long ears flipped this way and that batting away a fly. The mini entered through the paddock door and headed to his stall. The pygmy goat joined him, even though he had a stall of his own.

"Good night, Piggles." She breathed in deep, looking at the barn with pleasure. It was kind of fun putting the zoo to bed.

The barn smelled like dust, hay, horse, and other good smells. So much better than that tractor shed she was going to finish tomorrow. The goose followed her around as she went to the stall where the goat had joined the mini.

"Gonna sleep with your good buddy, Bob?" Sunny rubbed the goat behind the ears. "Don't worry, I'll remember to shut the barn door," she told Which Way, who was unconvinced and kept following her. She snuggled her head onto the top of the platinum silver mane of the mini. "What *is* your name?"

The mini snorted, threw back his head, and sniffed her ear for treats. She let out her own snort.

"How 'bout Wuffle for a name?" The mini looked away. "No, huh? I'll give you a rocko-socko name; don't worry." She talked to herself as she closed the barn door. "I'm closing the barn door, guys. You all see me do it, right?"

She would be a finisher. Just wait and see.

Chapter 12

What Am I Good For?

Wednesday seemed like two days glued together and each a hundred hours long. Sunny's alarm went off—three times—until Uncle Dave's hoarse voice yelled down the hall, "Turn that thing off or get up!"

In the living room, she spilled the water glass for his pain medicine and had to mop it up with a towel from the bathroom because she hadn't unpacked the kitchen towels yet. When she opened the barn door, the zoo was already in the paddock through the paddock door— that she'd, um, forgotten to close the previous night.

"You're doing a great job, Sunny." Uncle Dave sat up on the couch, bleary eyed, as she brought him lunch.

Good thing you can't walk right now. You might say something different.

After schoolwork was done, Sunny brushed the mini and the goat, led them out to the corral behind the house, and twisted the spigot to fill the water trough. As soon as she unclipped the goat's lead in the corral, he scooted on his knees under the rail, hightailing it to the front. When he stopped at the oval and started to graze, she walked back to the corral. Pulling an Esther pose, she placed her hands on her hips and addressed the pig and the goose that had waddled from the barn.

"You guys can come and go as you please. Just don't make me chase you!"

With a couple of flaps, the goose was splashing and honking in the half-filled water trough. The pig found an old garden in the shade to the left of the corral and began to root a row in it.

"Well, someone could adopt Piggles and he can root up their garden in the spring," Sunny said to the mini. She turned to the other animals. "What are you all good at?" It looked like Bob was going to be good at mowing.

Her question reflected her own problem. She'd been good at Great Ideas. *Been* good at them.

No matter. She'd get used to not having Great Ideas. She would simply have to find something else she was good at.

Back to school stuff. She caught up on the assignments she was behind in and video chatted with her mother and told her everything was going fine. She talked to Uncle Dave until he fell asleep.

Then she counted the hours until the Squad would arrive. She thought of the tractor shed a few times while she opened the endless boxes and put things away. Uncle Dave groggily said he did not care where things went as long as kitchen stuff landed in the kitchen, bathroom stuff in the bathroom, and so on. It seemed the pile of boxes would never go down. Some boxes were marked SHED. She groaned. Like the shed needed more stuff in it.

Taking a break in the afternoon, she wandered toward the corral. The water trough was running over and, from the looks of the mucky mini, the goopy goose, and the oh-so-happy pig in mud, it had been on since—

"Ughness!" Sunny slogged through the mud and turned off the spigot. "Great, just great." No point in taking off her sneakers to save them; they were toast. She led the muddy trio back to the tractor shed for another hosing. Bob the goat was making great progress on the oval.

Finally, finally, after hosing off her own sneakers, going into the house, seeing the track of barefoot mud she'd left, wiping up the tracks, and sighing *mightily*, she heard a vehicle pull into the circular driveway. Getting a good hold on the front door, she yanked on it and pushed open the screen with both hands.

The Squad had arrived!

They unpacked a few more boxes and did their homework. Too soon the girls had to leave, and Sunny began a new countdown to the next day after school.

That's when Esther would be staying overnight!

Chapter 13

A Creepy Feeling

The zoo was out of the barn and running in every direction except the same. Sunny darted one way and then another, yet every time she nearly touched one of them, they squirted out of her hand. Then the pig began to fly, and the mini horse said, "Come here so I can stomp on your foot!"

Sunny sat up, her heart pounding in her throat, sleep as well as the dream vibrating in her brain. Where was she? Right. She was in her bed at Uncle Dave's. Thursday night; Esther lay curled up on the inflatable mattress. Through the open window, the dark sky above the corral and meadow said nighttime. A chilly breeze blew, but it wasn't as cold as Sunny felt when she saw a shape outlined through the window.

She burrowed back under the covers. She did not see something at the window. What a crazy dream. She must still be dreaming. A sweaty moment later, she peeked out. No doubt about it. Something was looking at her from the open window.

"Esther! Esther, wake up!" Loud enough for her friend to hear, low enough that—that—thing couldn't.

Esther stirred.

The shadowy figure snorted. Just like—

Sunny bounded out of bed. Now she could see the ears. It was the mini. She leaned through the window. There, below the view of the window was Piggles, Bob, and Which Way. Which Way looked very pleased with himself.

"How did you—?"

The zoo had been safely in the barn with the door shut. She'd shut it right after dinner while Esther did the dishes. Honest. They were safe.

No, they were looking in her window.

But she *had* shut the barn door, hadn't she? She'd gone through Vee's checklist and actually checked everything off and—

She smacked her forehead with her hand. She'd left the list and the pen in the barn. It had all the instructions for Uncle Dave Mom had left that Vee had written in her perfect handwriting. She needed that notebook 'cause it also included all *her* lists on how to care for the animals and how to split up the chores.

She'd better go get it and check the door, just to make sure. She would also check to see how the zoo got out. No way did she want to mess up her chance to prove to her family that she could finish things.

"Okay, guys, lemme get dressed and I'll be out."

Yawning, she checked the bedside clock. With the ranch away from city lights, night was really *night*. A flashlight would be handy, but that would have been something Esther or Vee would have remembered, she reflected, slipping her feet into a pair of flip-flops and pulling on a sweatshirt. A sigh over leaving the handy-dandy list in the barn. Reinventing herself as Vee wasn't going to work.

"The trouble with a list is you have to remember where you put the list," she muttered, opening the bedroom door.

Esther slowly sat up, stretching. After a quick look out the window, she whispered, "I see ears. Is that the mini? It's not morning yet. What are you doing?"

"I'm going to see how they got out. I'm sure I closed the door." Her voice lowered. "I also forgot the list in the barn. I'm going to get it."

In seconds, Esther had rolled off the bed. "Let me get my flashlight out of my backpack. Then we can go."

I knew it.

Dressing quickly and digging out her big-ended flashlight, Esther was ready to go. Crossing to the window and sitting on her rear and rolling out, a twinge of guilt zinged Sunny. It would be longer now for Uncle Dave to screen the windows and everything else on his "I've got to look at that" list.

As soon as Sunny was out the window, the mini moved in for an ear wuffle. "Maybe your name should be Magician," Sunny said, rubbing him behind the ears. He drew back his head and shook it. "Okay. I'll keep trying."

The two girls stood for a moment in the cool-but-not-cold air with their heads thrown back, marveling at the stars. So many more than she saw at home. Sunny spun from sheer joy. Here she was, free and outdoors in the freaky weather of November. The zoo must be magicians because she was *sure* she'd shut the barn door. She skipped toward the corner of the house, throwing in a little spin every few skips. Okay, so being Vee wasn't going to work, being helpful like Aneta hadn't worked. Esther jogged next to her.

Rounding the corner and crunching as quietly as possible, so as not to awaken Uncle Dave, the two approached the nighttime hulk of the barn.

"I bet you did close the door," Esther said. "They must have found another way out."

Esther was a good friend.

Right after Esther finished speaking, the back of Sunny's neck began to prickle like it did when she knew her brothers were sneaking around to jump out and scare her. Sunny didn't scare easily, but not *seeing* the danger and just *feeling* the danger was, well, creepy. Looking around on full alert, she slowed to careful steps so her flip-flops wouldn't crunch the gravel. *Neck still prickling here.*

Esther walked so close she might as well have been in Sunny's pocket. In a low mutter, she said, "Do you feel like someone is watching us?"

"Yes." Sunny mumbled the word out of the corner of her mouth. "Maybe it's because it's so dark?"

Arriving at the barn door, Sunny's heart sank.

The barn door was open.

Not a lot, but definitely not closed with the long bolt shot down through the two iron rings.

Ughness.

And worse, the tingly feeling intensified.

"Is—is—anybody there?" Esther tried to sound tough and loud.

Sunny thumped her on the arm. "You don't say that!" Her voice rasped with fear. "What if somebody *is* there?"

Esther hunched her shoulder to the ear where Sunny's whisper had been more like a shriek. "Ow. Okay." She looked around, too. "I don't see anyone." She shivered. "I—I just feel like we're being watched."

Sunny blew out a bubbling breath of relief and hysteria. "We are."

Esther gasped. "Where?"

Sunny pointed back from where they'd come. In a straggly line the zoo stood silhouetted against the dark of the meadow. "But you know, I *know* I closed the door. Tight. I told Which Way I was closing the door. He saw me. I mean, I forgot the list and pen, but I did finish closing up the barn."

Esther turned in a slow circle, eyes squinting, checking the outbuildings and the field that extended beyond the back corral. She surveyed the driveway in front of the house. "Bob's almost finished the oval," she observed. "I don't see anybody."

Sunny ducked into the barn thinking about the zoo. Piggles excelled at digging gardens. Bob mowed weeds. What about Which Way and the mini? *What about* me *now that I don't have Great Ideas?* She must keep trying. She had one Squader left to imitate. It would involve being bossy and getting people to finish things.

The list was right where she thought it would be. As she walked out, Piggles, Bob, Which Way, and the mini—what *was* that horse's name?—walked into the barn as though someone were leading them with invisible leashes.

"So do you think we were imagining things?" Esther asked as the two girls walked quietly back to the window.

Sunny's neck had ceased to prickle. "Yeah." Once Esther had tumbled herself into the bedroom, Sunny placed both hands on the sill, bounced, and tipped over the edge. She wriggled a bit more and fell onto the floor with a clunk.

"Shhh! You'll wake your uncle!" Esther helped her up. "You still have the list?"

Yes, Esther was good at being bossy. Pulling it from her pocket, Sunny laid it on the dresser. "Trying to be Vee didn't work. I forget the stuff to be organized." She flopped on her bed. "Now I'm really sleepy. Good night, Esther." Already her eyes felt like bags of sand pressed them down. The sheets were cool and smooth. Her voice began to drag. "Tomorrow I'll be bossy. Maybe that's me."

No response from the other girl, although Sunny heard her lie down on the mattress.

She murmured to Esther. "You did see me close the door the second time, right?"

Esther huffed and flopped over so her back was to Sunny.

What's the matter with her?

Chapter 14

Why Is Esther Mad?

The next morning when the alarm sounded, Esther rolled off the mattress, dressed quickly, and flounced out of the room without a word. She didn't look at Sunny either.

Why isn't Esther talking? Sunny was moving a bit slower after their late night. Mom called this "stupid thirty" in the morning. Why did animals have to eat breakfast so early? Sunny yawned, leaning over to tie still-wet sneakers. Today she would make a stupendous breakfast for her uncle. He hadn't been eating much. Maybe today he wouldn't have to take pain pills so she could finally tell him about the temporary zoo in the tractor shed. Once he knew, and knew they would look for homes, they could begin.

Rather than make her happy, the thought saddened her. Having the mini follow her around and wuffle in her ear was pretty great. She was sure, however—as sure as she had burned yesterday's dinner—that her parents would *never* go for a mini horse in their backyard.

Still yawning, she stood up, thinking about what she had to finish today. She and Esther would hustle through the chores and attack their schoolwork. That had been one of the rules when Esther's mom had said she could stay with Sunny rather than attend her school's service project day. "School has to be done," she'd said.

"Oh yes," Mom had agreed, shooting Sunny a look. "Sunny's going to be diligent to get hers finished as well."

Once school got out, Vee and Aneta would join them for the whole weekend. One of them would figure out why Esther was ignoring Sunny. She stepped to the window. Esther stood on the ground outside, an odd look on her face.

"Sunny."

Good. Esther wasn't mad anymore. Whatever she *had* been mad about, Sunny had no idea. They'd climbed out a window, freaked each other out with thinking someone was watching them, closed the barn door, and gone to bed. Where could Esther have gotten mad?

"You're talking to me now?" she teased, grabbing a sweatshirt from the floor and pulling it over her head.

Esther placed her hands on her hips. "I'm only talking to you this once to let you know there's a horse out there."

Sunny chuckled. "There's three. Shirley, Mondo, and the mini. Two and a half if you count that the mini is a mini."

The hands turned to fists. "I *know* there were three horses. Now there are *four*."

Sunny sat on the sill and swung her legs out. "Maybe you just counted wrong 'cause you're not used to seeing horses." She landed on the ground and wiped her hands on the back of her capris.

"I just remembered I'm not talking to you," Esther said, zooming past her along the side of the house. "And I *know* how to count."

Sunny came around the corner, breathing a sigh of relief that the barn door remained closed. Then she noted movement in the first corral. A brown horse with a black mane and tail was chasing around the biggest soccer ball Sunny had ever seen.

Chapter 15

Sunny Gets It Wrong

Whoa," Sunny said. She and Esther stood together. Esther still had her hands on her hips. "How did you get here?" she asked the horse. The animal noticed them and came up to the rail, stuck his neck over, and sniffed their hands. Black lashes longer than the mini's framed the brown eyes, and a well-combed forelock partially covered a jagged white blaze down the long nose. Its tail was also well brushed.

Sunny took a step nearer. The horse nickered. She reached out to get a velvet nose and prickly whiskers in her hand. She hunched her shoulders. "I don't think he's mean. I wonder how he got lost?"

"You can't get lost and put yourself in a corral if you're a horse, Sunny." Yep, Esther was still mad about whatever.

Keeping a careful distance from the watchful horse, Sunny bent and peered through the rails. "Esther! Check out that giant ball!"

"Did you bring your own toy?" Esther directed her question to the brown horse while Sunny opened the barn door to release Shirley and Mondo into their adjoining corral. They exchanged nose bumps with the mysterious horse over the dividing rails.

"I know Uncle Dave wouldn't put a strange horse in with his

secondhand horses right away," Sunny said. "So we won't."

The brown horse walked to the hayrack in the corner and nosed it. Now Sunny noticed the ribs on the dull brown hide. "He's hungry!"

"I'll get some hay, Mr. Horse." Esther backed away from where she'd been leaning her elbows on the railing and dashed into the barn. She reappeared a few moments later, arms full of hay. "I couldn't carry a whole bale."

"I can't either. They weigh eighty pounds."

"I'm not talking to you. I'm talking to the horse."

Sunny felt like she'd been hit with a test on a subject she'd never studied. What was Esther's deal?

"Well, Uncle Dave's gonna have a surprise when he wakes up." Sunny twirled a piece of her hair. "And this time it's not my fault." She looked at Esther. "And why aren't you talking to me?"

Esther faced Sunny. "You called me bossy. That's not very nice."

"I didn't call you bossy." Sunny twisted her mouth as she mentally scurried through the previous evening. When had she said Esther was bossy?

"You just about did. You said that being Vee didn't work because you left the list in the barn. You said you were going to try to be like me and be bossy. Right before you went to sleep."

Color and heat poured into Sunny's face. Oh. *That* comment. "I—I just meant that you finish things and tell people what to do and they—do it. Except maybe for Vee when she wants to be the one to tell people to do stuff. . ." Her voice trailed off. Esther's face had transformed from an angry flush to madly blinking. Had she made her friend *cry*?

"Esther! I'm sorry. I'm so sorry!" She stepped forward and threw her arms around her friend. Esther burst into tears. "I'm so mean. I didn't mean it in a bad way. Oh, the *ugh*ness of it all!"

Peering at her through her tears, Esther sucked in a shuddery breath. "Oh, Sunny! You and your sayings."

Sunny squeezed her friend tightly and released her. "Yeah, it's like the opposite of yayness, I guess. It's been a lot of ughness around here with me and my Great Ideas." She repeated her apology, and Esther accepted.

"Now, let's go make breakfast for your uncle and let him know he has another secondhand horse. Let's hope he hasn't taken any medicine lately."

The two girls linked arms and began an awkward skip back to the house, hee-heeing as they lurched into one another. "I don't think he'll mind. Shirley and Mondo are secondhand horses, and Uncle Dave said he was building his horse ranch. Now he's got four—well, three and a half—secondhand horses. He'll have to get a sign that says Secondhand Ranch."

Esther chuckled over the reference to the mini. "Wait till we tell Vee and Aneta about the creepy feeling last night and the door being open and the zoo outside the window and now this mysterious horse. . . ." She sighed. "I so love being a Squader."

The girls together put their shoulders to the front door and fell into the kitchen.

Over a breakfast of scrambled eggs only slightly brown, bacon that was just perfect, and toast with chunks of butter because Sunny had forgotten to leave it out the night before, the two girls explained how the Squad had purchased the zoo. They also learned that no, Uncle Dave had not taken any pain medicine yet and yes, he had quite a different idea for his horse ranch. One that did not include a zoo or additional secondhand horses.

"You bought a zoo? Someone abandoned a horse here? I'm calling the sheriff." He reached for the phone and groaned. "Dagnabbit, any time I move, this stupid ankle hurts. Sunny, hand me the phone, will you?"

"Why would someone do that, Mr. Martin?" Esther asked.

He shrugged, letting the phone fall into his lap. "Lots of reasons. Maybe they're moving and can't take the horse. Mostly it's because people have run out of money. Sometimes it's a choice between paying the mortgage or taking care of the horse." He glanced at Esther's indignant face. "They're not bad people, Esther. Sometimes they get overwhelmed. Taking care of a horse is a big responsibility in terms of time and money."

Sunny shifted in her chair. This conversation was not going exactly the way she would've liked. "Uncle Dave, I'm sorry I couldn't tell you about the zoo sooner. Mom said to wait until you were off the pain meds. And I'm sorry about your ankle. And so sorry I didn't clean the outbuilding." *Which I still haven't. Sunneeee!* "I thought since you had secondhand horses and were talking to someone on the phone about a mare, you were getting more secondhand horses."

"On the phone?" Uncle Dave's brow cleared. "That was a breeder. I'm going to start a sport pony ranch. Very high-end. No more secondhand horses for me."

Sunny gulped. She'd been wrong all the way around. Her Great Idea of buying the zoo had been a Great Mistake. So had her Great Idea that her uncle would be okay with owning a zoo. "Okay." Her voice trembled, but she tried to steady it. "The Squad will find homes for all of them. Or"—she brightened—"we'll find a way to have the zoo make money to help take care—"

Her uncle rubbed his face. "No, Sunny." His voice sounded as tired as his face looked. "Finding homes for the zoo, yes. Trying to find a way to make money with the zoo? No way. That's one of your great ideas I have no interest in." Opening the pill bottle on the table next to him, he took one out, grimaced, and put it back. "A miniature horse? Now that's a minor horse. What good is a miniature horse? You can't ride it. It can't pull a plow." He sighed. "Now it's time for me to take a rest."

A few minutes later, as Esther and Sunny stood in the kitchen, breakfast dishes in the sink, boxes still crowding the room, Sunny heard Uncle Dave's slow, deep breathing on the couch. Esther was chewing her lip and avoiding looking at Sunny.

Sunny heaved a sigh that filled her lungs and left her dizzy on the exhale. "For pizza sake, me and my Great Ideas. Uncle Dave wants to breed horses, not rescue ones that are already alive." Deep inside, somehow, she was disappointed in Uncle Dave.

Esther slid an arm around her friend's shoulders and squeezed. "Okay, so we can't make up stuff to have the zoo earn money. We've adopted out dogs and cats. We'll let people know what the zoo is good at. In fact," she said, her serious face beginning to relax, "we already know Piggles is good at gardens. Bob is good at mowing." She started toward the sink. "Now we need to find out what the goose and the mini are good at."

Staring off into space, Sunny nodded. "Yeah." She kind of felt like the zoo. What good was she? She knew from years of Sunday school that God loved everyone. That He didn't make mistakes creating people; however, she wasn't *quite* sure He hadn't dozed off when He was finishing *her* brain. After all, He had done an *awful* lot of creating.

Uncle Dave thought she couldn't finish anything and that her Great Ideas *weren't*. What good was a mini horse? She gritted her back teeth and made herself spin. She would make the zoo adoptions the best thing. She would show him the "minor" mini could do something major. She'd remember to take out the butter the night before, for pizza sake. For the zoo, she had to come up with an idea. Not a Great

Idea. *No more Great Ideas.* Simply an idea she could finish. The sooner she practiced being Esther, the better.

The girls cleaned up the kitchen and settled in with their schoolwork. Esther sat on the front porch and did her math while Sunny attended one of her online history classes. Medieval times. Not her favorite. They took the rest of the schoolwork out to the corral and read their assignments to the horses. The zoo insisted on attending, all-attentive with wuffles, bleats, honks, and grunts. Esther said they ought to allow animals in schools to make schoolwork more fun. Sunny agreed.

With the final work checked off and a video chat to Sunny's mom to let her know, the two headed out to play with the zoo. Only the mini was interested. Bob wanted to finish chomping on the oval. Which Way was lying next to Piggles, who was in his favorite shady, dusty place. They politely asked the mystery horse they'd named Mystery—of course—if they could borrow the ball, then took the ball and the mini to the back corral that had nearly dried out from the mud party. Piggles and Which Way followed then headed toward the remaining mud.

When the mini stood shoulder to ball, the ball was taller.

"Are you sure you can do this? You're awfully small," Sunny said. Would this be one more thing a mini couldn't do that a "real" horse could?

He flickered an eye as if to say, "Watch me!" First he looked at it. Then he nosed it, crow hopping backward as it rolled. Sunny laughed until tears leaked out of her eyes. In the next moments, as he grew braver, he dashed straight at it until the girls gasped for fear he would roll right up and down the other side. At the last moment, he swerved and gave it a kick with a back leg on the way by.

Which Way waddled out of the mud to see what was happening. He missed death on numerous occasions by flying into the corral during the mini's mad charge. This went on long enough that Sunny forgot everything else. The mini was *fun*.

Finally, Sunny remembered the tractor shed.

"C'mon, Esther," she said. They left the mini intent on his game.

Standing in the shed doorway, they peered into the gloom, stripes of light beaming in from the long, jagged gaps in the shrunken wooden roof.

"This place is truly creepy," Esther said, making no move to go farther. "No wonder we felt like someone was watching us."

"And dangerous," Sunny reminded her. "Watch where you step. Let me prop both doors open." The rest of the Squad would be there shortly. Time to practice telling the girls the way to clean out the shed. Maybe she was a bossy type. It sure worked for Esther. Knocking over a rusty oilcan as she ventured farther in, she bent down to inspect it. She pulled the trigger. Amber oil squirted out.

"Huh." The barn doors could use a bit of this.

At the barn, she eyed the hinges. Where to shoot it? *Squirt.* Whoa. That was a lot.

"You're supposed to oil the hinges, not drown them," Esther said from behind her, critically regarding the operation.

Tires crunched, and Esther squealed. "It's Vee and Aneta!"

Sunny dropped the oilcan.

"We have so much to tell you!" Esther screeched as Vee and Aneta tumbled out of Aneta's mom's SUV. "I thought Aneta's grandmother was bringing you guys."

Ms. Jasper stepped out of the driver's side wearing a suit that made her look like she should be the president. Her hair, blond and long, fell neatly from a clip. She smiled at the girls. "I thought I'd drop off some of Gram's special treats and my peanut butter cookies for Sunny's uncle."

For a tiny second, a second so fast it might not have happened, Sunny thought Aneta's mom's face turned pink. Why would Ms. Jasper's face get red? It was a sunny day, but not a hot-summer-sun kind of day. Just sweatshirt on, sweatshirt off kind of day. Weird.

Aneta and Vee walked into the house with Esther and Sunny, dropped off their backpacks, pillows, and stuffed animals in the bedroom, and then ran out to the corral to say hello to Mystery, Shirley, and Mondo. They waved to Bob who watched them while chewing a weed. On the way to the back corral, they greeted Piggles with a snort that caused him to snort. Then they were at the corral where Which Way was still getting in the way of the mini playing ball.

"I love it, I love it!" Vee yelled, clapping her hands. "It's more fun than TV. That ball is *splendiferous!*"

"He is having so much fun with it," Aneta said, her grin wide.

Sunny and Esther filled in the other two with the news—the appearance of the bay horse and the gigantic ball. Uncle Dave had made calls, but no one knew where he came from. Sunny figured Mystery had arrived so the girls would have another horse to ride. Immediately after that, they moved on to the *really* exciting news: they thought they'd surprised a burglar the previous night.

"Oh no! Were the animals all right?" Aneta's blue eyes widened.

"You didn't catch even a smidge of the person?" Vee asked.

With the mini following the ball Sunny rolled, Which Way and the girls walked the drive back to the front corral. Mystery, Shirley, and Mondo were nuzzling each other across the fence that separated them.

"How come that new horse can't be in with Shirley and Mondo?" Aneta climbed up to sit on the top rail of the corral corner, close to the three horses. "They are friends already."

Sunny opened her mouth to answer when Aneta's mom joined

them. "Just like you wouldn't put dogs who don't know each other together, it's the same with any animal. You have to see what's going on with the horse." She flopped her arms over the top rail and surveyed the new horse. "This one looks like it's used to being around other horses. You girls said it was just here this morning when you came out?"

Sunny and Esther nodded.

Ms. Jasper shook her head. "It's not right to abandon a horse. It's against the law." She walked into the barn and emerged with a long blue lead. Ducking between the rails, she slowly approached the horse, talking soothingly.

"Mom!" Aneta's gasp carried across the corrals. "What are you *doing*?"

"Um. . ." Sunny felt panic rising up. How about what Ms. Jasper just said about being careful with horses you don't know? "Does your mom know anything about horses?"

"I do not know."

Sunny truly, *truly* hoped Aneta's mom knew what she was doing. Sunny just couldn't see herself taking care of one more patient.

Chapter 16

Not Esther Either

You just never know about parents.

Along with Sunny, Vee, and Esther, Aneta found out her mother had ridden quite a bit from when she was Aneta's age all the way through college. She'd even won awards! *I think she knows as much as Uncle Dave about horses.* Margo Jasper made the girls laugh when she led Mystery to the living room window to allow Uncle Dave to see if he recognized him. He agreed with her that the horse seemed safe to put in with Shirley and Mondo.

More yayness than that was she received permission from Uncle Dave to start riding lessons with the girls. All four of them did a happy dance holding hands. Once again, Sunny remembered the tractor shed. For pizza sake, that shed was like a splinter you couldn't get out. Always bothering you. No more putting it off.

About two hours later, Sunny surveyed the tractor shed with some pride and a great deal of thankfulness for her friends. The shed, where Uncle Dave had met his horrible fate, had a cracked cement floor you could *see*. Sure, a few chunks were missing and there were lots of cracks, but yes, there was a floor. It wasn't a Great Idea and it wasn't exciting or fun, but it was working.

What wasn't working, however, was being good at being Esther. Sunny tried telling everyone what to do. Except she kept forgetting to think ahead to the next thing, and the girls kept coming up and asking, "Where does this go? What do I do with this?" Finally, she burst out with, "Okay, I'm not a good Esther. Everybody, do what you want. Just make it so"—she made an exaggerated sweep of her hand to include the entire shadowy, cluttered shed—"nobody"—she winced—"and I mean *nobody*, will trip over anything."

"I could take over and tell everyone," Esther offered.

"I can figure it out. Thanks, Esther." Vee grabbed an open, dried-out paint can, tucked a canning jar of nails and screws under her arm, and began to drag an old carpet toward the shed door.

Esther huffed, looked like she might get mad—Sunny hoped she wouldn't—then shook her head. "Okay, here we go! Operation Clean!" Bending over, she inspected a rusted, dented bucket. "There's a pair of spurs in here."

Sunny told her how those spurs had sent her sprawling her first night at the ranch.

"Ugh. They're, like, sharp and dangerous and rusty." Holding them as if they were bombs about to go off, Esther returned them to the bucket.

Once everything was out, the girls sorted it into piles. Vee's idea: Junk, which meant it got dumped in the Dumpster on the far side of the lean-to; Keep (Esther's insistence), which meant it was placed in the back left corner (Esther and Aneta's job); and Who Knows?, which meant they would have to ask Uncle Dave when he was next awake. Sunny did whatever she was told.

Aneta and Sunny stacked the Who Knows? pile in the back corner, way out of the way. This included the yoke that had trapped and snapped Uncle Dave's ankle. Sunny shuddered as she dragged it to the back.

"Not much time left." In the doorway, Vee stood silhouetted by the fading light of day. "How much is there left to do?"

"No time for the top floor." Sunny blew out a tired breath. "I don't think I'll be going up there anytime soon anyway. You guys, if I had to do this by myself, I would be doing it until my brothers were taller than I am." She kicked the stack of old metal buckets. "Thanks BUCKETS. So you think maybe it was a Great Idea that I *didn't* do it when Uncle Dave asked me? So I'd have help?" She sucked in her cheeks so she wouldn't laugh.

"Ha-ha, I don't think so," Vee said sternly.

"My mom would say two wrongs don't make a right!" Esther shook her head as a smile slipped out.

"Sunny!" Aneta looked horrified, yet a grin slid over her face.

"Joking! Joking!" She couldn't keep her face looking serious. "I'm starving. Oh no!" Turning a shocked face toward her friends, she said, "I forgot to feed Uncle Dave. If it's dark, it must be past suppertime."

"You need to feed us, too," Vee reminded her.

After a hilarious dinner with Uncle Dave, who was wide awake, the girls spent the rest of the evening unpacking his boxes. He sat up on the couch so he could direct their efforts, his ankle supported on pillows. With their running in and out of rooms, yelling, "Here? Does it go here?" the pile of boxes shrank. Uncle Dave seemed to be enjoying the job, Sunny thought. His rat-a-tat laugh was back.

This was the most fun unpacking had ever been. Her uncle had some weirdo cool stuff from his travels around the country and was more than willing—now that he was off pain pills—to tell the story behind it. With another box nearly emptied, she peered in to see what was left. One cowboy boot with a glitter-covered fake plant sticking out. "Wow, Uncle Dave. What's the story with this ugly thing? Glitter and cowboy boots don't go together!" Taking the few steps into the sitting room, she stood before her uncle, dangling the boot from a strap.

The smile that had been tickling around her uncle's mouth as he teased the girls through their work vanished, as though Sunny had taken an eraser and wiped it out.

"You can throw that out." He frowned. "I thought I had a long time ago." His eyes looked worser than before, Sunny thought, dumping the boot in the big trash can. *Worser* was a word her little brother used. Sad eyes. They looked different than pain eyes. This was a story her uncle didn't want to tell. Soon after, he said he was ready to stop thinking about unpacking.

Vee, after surveying the remaining boxes, asked him if it was okay if they set up the boxes in the kitchen. "I helped my mom set up the kitchen when we moved into Bill's house. Bill said I did a bang-up job."

Uncle Dave looked at her then at Sunny. Sunny, with shame rushing up the back of her neck and staining her cheeks, knew he must be thinking Vee had Great Ideas and was a finisher.

"Vee *always* finishes," she said, choking a little on the clutch in the back of her throat. "Not like me."

Uncle Dave winked at Sunny. "Nice to have friends, huh? Okay, Vee, go ahead. I'm no gourmet cook anyway. Just tell me where everything is."

Vee stepped over to the table and waved a pack of sticky notes. "I brought these. We'll mark every drawer and cupboard after we're done. No problem."

Esther patted Vee on the back. "Vee's organized. So am I."

"Just so you know, Uncle Dave," Sunny hastened to add, "I'm working on finishing things. I tried to be like Aneta and be helpful with your pillows, but—"

"Glad you left that for Aneta," was her uncle's dry remark.

"Then I made lists like Vee. Only—" She remembered the slightly opened barn and that she hadn't told her uncle yet. She hurried to finish. "Only I left it in the barn and had to go get it with Esther. The door was a teeny bit open—"

"Good thing you left the list in the barn." Uncle Dave inched forward on the couch, positioned the crutches on either side of him, and pulled himself up. "Otherwise, forgetting to close the barn door could have been serious." He took two steps and winced. "Ow. What's that word I hear you saying? Ughness. That's what this is." With that, he hobbled down the hall to his room.

"Only, I *didn't* leave the door open. . . ," Sunny began, but Uncle Dave was muttering under his breath. She caught a few words.

". . .so sure I'd gotten rid of that years ago. Like I need to re-member *her*."

Forty-five minutes later, the girls had cleared the boxes and filled nearly all the cupboards and drawers until only a box of mismatched glasses was left.

Sunny pushed open the screen door to add another empty box to the pile Mom and Dad would take to the recycling place. She inhaled a deep breath. It smelled like—well, a ranch. Horses. The three and a half horses nickered to one another. The mini threw in an extra one to let her know he had seen her and wanted his ears rubbed. Three big. Then a dip to a little shadow with pricked up ears. Swirling all the way through the horsiness, the smell of pine trees, grass, and animals.

As she entered the kitchen, she heard Esther.

"Glasses go in the cupboard by the dishwasher 'cause it's faster to put them away." Esther's fists were firmly planted. Yep. On her hips.

"No, they go by the sink because that's where people go get a drink of water. *Everybody* knows that." Vee made it sound like *anyone* with *half* a brain would know that.

Uh-oh. Sunny was actually surprised they'd gotten this far without an argument.

"You guys," she said helplessly, standing near the door.

Aneta opened the top drawer—which Vee and Esther had agreed should be the silverware drawer—and removed a fork and spoon. She held both behind her back. Sunny saw her stick the spoon into her back pocket. What was Aneta up to?

"We will decide," the blond girl said in her quiet voice, slicing through the increasing volume of Vee and Esther. "Sunny's uncle is sleeping, so we do not yell."

"I'm not yelling. Esther is the one who's yelling," Vee said, but lowered her voice.

This remark pulled Esther's face into downturned lips and narrowed eyes.

Oh, for pizza sake.

"What do I have in my hand—a fork or a spoon?" Aneta asked, her voice showing her smile. Sunny watched. "If you guess what I have in my hand, you decide which cupboard the glasses go in. Then we are done, and we are the Squad again."

The girls each guessed eagerly, and Aneta removed the fork from behind her back. "Esther decides."

Vee rolled her eyes and began to laugh, leaning against the counter. "Aneta, you are so funny. Sorry, Esther."

Esther's face lightened into a full-faced grin.

Aneta sighed deeply. "So, we are the Squad again? I hope so."

Sunny walked to the middle of the girls and held out her right arm where the Squad bracelet encircled her wrist. The girls joined with theirs.

"The Squad!" they said, only very quietly so as not to wake Uncle Dave. "Together!"

"Let's go to bed," Sunny added.

Chapter 17

This Time Maybe?

The next morning, the S.A.V.E. Squad converged on their "official" meeting spot, the children's section of the Oakton Community Library.

"Sunny!" Nadine's cheerful face, framed by long black hair and bangs, greeted her. "Your mom and brothers have been in. I've missed your smiling face and your great ideas." Nadine stopped stacking books on her big desk and reached out to hug Sunny and then the others. Nadine and her husband, Frank, were good friends of the Squad, even if Frank tried to act like the girls were too much drama. "How come you're in town, ranch hand?"

"Dad came out to visit Uncle Dave, so Mom came too and brought me to Esther's house. Then we walked over." Sunny surveyed the colorful banners overhead waving in the air currents. "It's been like forever since we've all been here together." She shot a rueful look at Nadine. "Except I don't have Great Ideas anymore. Now I try to finish things."

"Why can't you do both?" A tall, skinny man with a ponytail walked through the children's section wearing a tool belt and carrying a bulging bag. Frank. Nadine's husband. . .and maintenance guy. . . and van driver for the community center. He glanced over at the girls, and his gaze settled on Sunny. "Been kind of quiet here without you girls."

Esther giggled. "I know you want to say 'without the drama,' Frank. Go ahead."

"Without the drama." He kept walking, not cracking a smile.

"You girls do know he adores you, right?" Nadine finished collecting her armful of short chapter books. "I don't want you to think he doesn't. Hey—you girls came at a good time. Adventure Readers reading club starts in a few minutes. Okay if you come talk to the kids about loving to read? You *are* the famous S.A.V.E. Squad. The kids are third, fourth, and fifth graders."

"Don't kids who come to the library already like to read?" Esther sounded surprised.

Sunny was surprised as well. Both her brothers devoured books. Her dad said the public library saved him from running out of room in the house *and* money to pay for books.

They were nearing the conference room where the reading group met. Nadine lowered her voice. "These are reluctant readers. For various reasons, they haven't yet seen how great reading is. Some don't read well; others don't have books at home or people who read aloud to them." She threw a glance at Sunny. "Got any great ideas on how to connect reading to kids?"

Aneta's soft voice was incredulous. "Not like to read? Oh, we will tell them how fun it is to read. I learned good English by reading girl detective stories when I was adopted by my mom."

Nadine introduced the girls and told the quiet group of three girls and five boys about how the girls met and about their first two adventures. Since some of the kids had been at the park during those times, they volunteered their memories with excitement. Once those stories were told, the children sent admiring looks toward the Squad. Then the Squad told about their favorite stories and how they loved to read.

Sunny noticed, however, that when Nadine began reading bits from her chosen books, the kids got restless. *Kind of like me in my online science class.*

At the end, Nadine asked the group to share why they liked or didn't like reading. Immediately hands shot up.

"It's okay, I guess."

"It's boring."

"I like movies better."

"The words move around."

"I don't see anything when I read."

As Sunny listened, she wondered about what sort of Great Idea Nadine wanted. What did Sunny know about making reading fun? She had always *liked* to read. While she sort of listened to Nadine, she slid into that place in her head that would get her a nudge from her friends and so missed the end of the club hour. She'd been thinking. . . . That day that she and Esther had done their schoolwork out loud in front of the animals. *Hmm.* It had been more fun than reading it to themselves.

The reading club filed out afterward, shyly waving. The girls waggled their fingers back. Sunny opened her mouth to tell Nadine the Great Idea. Then she snapped it closed. Nope. Not this time. Wasn't she done with Great Ideas? Hadn't they gotten her in trouble?

Outside the library, Vee, Esther, and Aneta gathered near Sunny.

"Okay, spill!" Vee said.

"What were you thinking about?" Esther asked, cocking her head with a wary look.

"Did you get a Great Idea?" Aneta asked eagerly.

"Can't tell yet. Gotta talk to Uncle Dave."

No matter how the girls begged and offered her more ice cream once they had all licked through ice cream cones at The Sweet Stuff, Sunny refused.

This time, if it was truly a Great Idea, she would do it right.

Back at the ranch, she cleared her idea with Uncle Dave, who said she was amazing. Dad looked skeptical. Now, more than ever, she must make this happen. *And finish.* Then everyone would see that her Great Ideas could work out.

Uncle Dave and Sunny shook hands. Deal.

On Tuesday after school, Sunny's mom drove out to the ranch with the S.A.V.E. Squad and their bikes crammed into the minivan. She visited with Uncle Dave—who protested he didn't need 24-7 care—while the girls clipped on helmets and rode to the library. There, they helped Nadine select a very special pile of books for a very special field trip on Wednesday. Vee, Esther, and Aneta figured out Sunny's Great Idea as soon as Nadine laid out the parameters for titles. Nothing like hearing your best friends say you're brilliant. It was a good day.

No Sweet Stuff today; afternoons were short and the light faded early, so bike riding had to be speedy. Back at the ranch, Aneta's mom had arrived and was inside talking to Uncle Dave. In their riding lesson, the girls took turns learning their "seat" (which made them smirk) on Shirley, Mondo, and Mystery, and then everyone departed, leaving Uncle Dave and Sunny.

"It would be handy to have one more secondhand horse so the Squad could all ride at once," she remarked while they ate dinner watching an old Western movie. "We just need one more."

Her uncle rolled his eyes at her. He had been spending a bunch of time on the phone. It wasn't going well, at least from the phone conversations she had overheard. Perhaps if she mentioned it nicely enough times, her uncle would see that a secondhand horse ranch—with its own petting zoo—was a more rocko-socko idea.

He pointed to the TV. "Here's the part where the hunted becomes the hunter. Love this part." It was a deliberate distraction, and Sunny knew it. *Okay, Uncle Dave, but don't think I'm forgetting this.* Uncle Dave loved Westerns. Although Sunny worried about the horses in the movies, she did like the good guys winning over the bad guys wanting to take over the town. "The good guy stops running from the bad guy"—Uncle Dave leaned forward on his couch—"and turns to chase him and fight."

Too bad nothing exciting like that happened anymore. The Squad would be great if a bad guy tried, say—her mind wandered—*to take over the ranch*. She could just imagine. . . .

"You all set for tomorrow?" he asked, rousing himself to head for bed at the end when justice had been restored and the bad guys caught.

"Yup. The kids will be here at four."

The Squad arrived one after another immediately after school, each still in school clothes.

"I could not take the time to go home and change," Aneta said in her uniform of plaid skirt, white button-front blouse, and navy school blazer. "I am too excited."

"Same here." Esther pulled the school T-shirt over her navy capris.

Vee agreed. "Except I wear the same thing whether I'm in school or not."

Half an hour later, the community center van rolled into the driveway. Sunny thought Bob the goat had done a fine job on the oval. Frank stepped from the driver's seat, and eight children climbed out.

"A ranch!" one said.

"Nuh-uh! A farm!" another corrected.

"I smell animal poo," said a third.

"Yep," Frank said with a sigh, helping out the last two. "My day to drive one zoo to see another."

His wife, already hugging the Squad, looked at him over her shoulder and laughed. Nadine almost always laughed when Frank pretended he didn't like his job. The girls and Nadine knew he loved it. Although the Squad *had* made him have doubts a time or two, Sunny thought. She hustled to get herself and the mini in position for their part of the Great Idea.

Once Nadine had the kids seated on blankets on the oval, Nadine rummaged in the giant cloth bag made out of an old coffee-bean sack. Setting aside something next to her, she pulled out a book. "*Petey the Pig Runs a Pizzeria,*" she announced. A few chortles and much squirming.

A few pages in, Nadine read a line from the book a little more loudly than the others.

"Showtime!" Sunny whispered. With the mini standing patiently beside her in a place Sunny had never thought she'd see a horse, she looked toward the barn. Right on cue, Vee's hand came through the barn doorway and tossed out some grain. Piggles emerged to begin snuffling his way toward Nadine.

"Look!" One of the girls, who had never said a word at the library club meeting, pointed at Piggles. "It's Petey from the book!"

Suddenly, everyone's attention was on Piggles as he reached the blanket. He had found the "something" Nadine had removed from her bag. He began to snuffle and eat happily.

"It's a real pig!"

"Can I touch it?"

"Hmm. Shall I read more about Petey the pig?" Nadine asked, as though a pig showing up when she was reading a pig story was completely natural.

"Yes!" The answer was loud.

Just. Like. She. Imagined.

"We can pretend that this piggy is Petey." The small, dark-haired girl with the glasses pushed them up on her nose. "It's like it's real."

"Petey's the biggest pig ever," squealed a boy.

Who cares if the kid thinks Piggles is Petey, Sunny thought, stroking the soft nose of the mini. This Great Idea was going, well, *great*.

When Nadine stopped again—strategically, the girls knew—there was an outcry for more of Petey. Piggles had finished his grain and had settled into the soft, inviting dust nearby.

On the second book, the kids looked expectantly at the barn, but Esther and Which Way appeared from *behind* them, from the left side of the house. Esther acted surprised that a story was being read about a goose when she—why, imagine that—just happened to be carrying *her* goose. They petted the goose. The rowdiest boy from the library took hold of the goose's foot, felt how warm it was, and said, "It's like it's on fire!"

The third book, about a little goat who ran away from home, had them begging Nadine to read faster; they were sure they were getting an animal "for reals" with each story. Aneta rolled the big ball out of the paddock, the pygmy goat behind it, until just before the blanket.

Then she let Bob take over. The goat chased after it, butting it with his head, and then walked on over to the blanket for ear scratches. Nadine didn't get too far in that book, but two of the kids said they were going to check it out at the library the next day. "Now I know how cool a goat is!"

Finally, it was time for the miniature horse story. That had been tougher, and Nadine had to go to a nearby larger library system to borrow a miniature horse story. Sunny had been listening to everything. At Nadine's now-familiar slightly louder voice on one line, Sunny pushed open the screen door and walked out on the porch with the mini's mini hooves clopping on the wood floor.

Chapter 18

Sunny Gets It Right

It's a little *horse*!"

"Coming out of a *house*!"

"Horses aren't supposed to live in houses!" The rowdy kid didn't know what to think of this.

"Ohhhhhh!"

As soon as the mini saw the children, he pulled away from Sunny and trotted over to the blanket. Nadine and Frank were smiling big smiles. *I mean, really, who doesn't love a cute little horse?* Sunny grinned as she picked up the lead and followed.

It was difficult for Nadine to keep reading about a miniature horse who saves the day, but she did. When her voice flowed over the kids' delight at the mini, the mini's ears perked up straight and he moved to her side, head dipping up and down as though he were reading along.

That dissolved everyone in laughter. The shy little girl clasped her hands and murmured to herself, "Oh, I wish I could read to him."

The mini had found what he was good for.

He was a reading horse.

It was already dark by the time the girls and Uncle Dave finished supper. The girls put the three and a half horses to bed as well as the zoo and gathered in the living room. Vee's mom would soon arrive to collect her daughter, Aneta, and Esther, even though the three begged to be allowed to stay over and skip school the next day.

"So then Nadine and Frank passed out books and all the kids read out loud." Sunny took a swallow of water. Uncle Dave had watched from the kitchen window for as long as he could stand then retired to the living room. He'd missed the best part, Sunny told him as she and the Squad sat in front of him sharing cookies for dessert. "You'll never guess what the mini did then."

"I hate guessing. Just tell me," her uncle said.

"As soon as he heard each kid begin to read, he walked over and lowered his head to their shoulder, like he was *listening*!"

"He was the big hit," Aneta said.

"Nadine wants Sunny to bring him to the library for the Adventure Readers' next meeting. Can she, Mr. Martin?" Esther asked.

"Who would have thought Minor the mini would be useful. I mean, you can't ride him, you can't plow with him—" Uncle Dave's tone was teasing.

"Yep." Sunny wasn't going to let him win. "He can't mow the oval or root up the back garden either. But he can be a reading horse and help kids learn to love reading. Ha!" Then a thought struck her. "And I think you should stop calling him Minor the mini. I think he has a name now."

The girls leaned toward her.

"Well?" Esther asked.

"Not Minor the mini. *Major* the reading mini!"

"Major?" Vee cocked her head to the side. "Yes, it's good."

"Major the reading mini!" Aneta clapped her hands. "Yes!"

"Another Great Idea, Sunny," Esther said, smiling as she uncrossed her legs to get more comfortable.

Uncle Dave tipped back his head and drilled out his rat-a-tat laugh. "You win, Sunny. The minor is now a Major! Maybe I should—"

A hoarse, nasal screeching from the direction of the barn interrupted his maybe.

"What was that?" Vee twisted toward the kitchen, placed her hands on the floor, and popped to her feet. At the kitchen window, she announced. "I see a light—like a flashlight. Someone's in the barn!"

Chapter 19

Which Way Sounds the Alarm

One after another, the girls covered the few steps to the front door.

"Hey, girls! Don't go running off half-cocked!" Uncle Dave hollered, grabbing for his crutches, but Sunny had already wrenched open the front door. She banged the screen door with her fist and cleared the steps, hitting the ground at a run. Should she yell? Stay quiet and hope to catch the intruder?

Her question was answered a second later when she heard the bitty goat bleat, "Baahhhhhb!"; heard a high, shrill male voice screaming, "No, no, stay away from me! Ahhhhhh!"; and a figure—who ran like a boy—beat feet out of the barn, the goose so close behind him with its neck and wings outstretched that the guy stumbled as the goose bit the calf of his leg.

"Stop!" Esther's biggest, bossiest voice bellowed behind as Sunny sprinted after the shadowy figure, who had made it past Uncle Dave's room and was heading for the pasture. She had to get him before he disappeared into those stands of trees where the girls played hide-and-shriek.

Pounding feet sounded behind her, and then it was Vee passing her. Of course it was. Vee was pouring it all on now. Arms were pumping, held close to her body, knees were up, and eyes were on the dark blob of the man. Sunny's heart felt like it would either pop out her armpit or out her throat. She came to a gasping halt. Esther joined her.

"Um," Esther said as Vee quickly shortened the distance between her and the intruder.

"Yeah?" Sunny raised her hands over her head like Vee had told her. It helped you catch your breath. "What?"

"Sunny." Turning, Esther looked worried. "What is Vee going to *do* when she catches him?"

Oh no! If the intruder would break into a barn, what would he do to an eleven-year-old girl who told him to stop? Even if Vee used her Twin Terror stepsister voice, what would the guy do? Stop and say, "Okay, kid, you got me. I'll follow you back to the police"?

For a long, paralyzing moment, the two girls stared both slack jawed and bug eyed at each other.

Then, "Vee!" They screamed their long-legged friend's name in unison and began running after her. "Stop! Stop! *Don't* catch him!"

"I see footprints. Bigger than the girls'." Sheriff John Bucholtz, who looked more like a pirate than a policeman, squatted and checked out the marks on the barn floor's collection of dust, sawdust, and straw. "The animals don't appear to be messed with." Casting a look around, he continued, "It's the rest of the barn he was after."

While the sheriff scrutinized each stall, Sunny and the girls scoured the corners for clues. They even climbed into the haymow. Nothing but hay and the rustle of mice. Backing slowly down the ladder, Sunny heard the sheriff add, "That goose ruined the intruder's plan, for sure. Nothing much better than a watch goose. They're nasty things when they're mad."

The last zoo member to show what it was made for. Now *she* was the only one who needed to know.

Out of the corner of her eye, Sunny saw Esther's mouth open and knew—just *knew*—Esther was going to tell the sheriff this was not the first time the intruder had tried to get into the barn. She caught the other girl's eye and shook her head a tiny bit. Though Esther frowned, she closed her mouth.

Sipping from the water bottle the girls had brought her, Vee shook her head. "I can tell you it was a guy, but he had on a dark hoodie with the hood up. Couldn't tell what color the hoodie was or anything. Shirt was hanging out, but I didn't really see what it looked like. Then these two"—she waved an arm at Esther and Sunny—"caught up to me and told me to stop chasing him. I *could* have caught him." She sucked more water.

When Sunny noticed Uncle Dave swaying on his crutches, she rushed over and put a hand on his arm. "You need to lay down, Uncle Dave. We'll have the sheriff come in and talk to you."

He didn't protest. Slowly, and with a few mutterings of Sunny's new favorite word *ughness*, her uncle made his way back to the house. Getting up the three stairs to the porch took some doing. Sunny could tell he was in a lot of pain. Anger at the intruder burned through her insides like a summer wildfire. Dumbhead crook. What could a barn full of a secondhand petting zoo hold for a criminal?

"I'll skip the couch. I just want to go to bed for a while." Uncle Dave continued moving toward his bedroom, forehead furrowed with pain.

Sunny settled him in his bed, adjusted his pillows, and then dashed to the kitchen. She took a glass from the cupboard by the dishwasher and dropped ice cubes into it before filling it with water. She hurried back, water sloshing over the top. Her uncle lay with his eyes closed, and for a moment she thought he'd already fallen asleep. Then his voice, low and scratchy with pain, caught her attention.

"You didn't forget to shut the barn door the first time it was open, did you." It wasn't a question. His eyes opened. He looked at her with that same look Mom had when trying to get the straight story from the brothers. The one that said, "Don't even *think* about not telling the truth."

It caught Sunny off guard. She'd thought that with his pain medicines, her uncle hadn't noticed much of what had been said or happened this last week and a half.

Vee, Esther, and Aneta crowded the doorway. The sheriff's SUV crunched out of the driveway.

So. If she told her uncle that he was right and she *hadn't* forgotten, he might think it was too dangerous for the girls to be out here anymore. That wouldn't work for Sunny. While she'd been standing next to the sheriff and using what her brother called "the eagle eye," she had seen something that everyone else had missed.

Another Great Idea was forming, and this one would prove once and for all that she, Sunny Quinlan, was good at Finishing. Two Great Ideas finished in one day. Yeah. That was her gift. Great Ideas.

While Sunny wondered how to answer, her uncle's eyelids began to flutter, and then he was out, breathing deeply. The hobbling had been too much for him.

Sunny motioned to the girls.

Around the big table, she stood while they sat. Leaning forward and pressing her palms on the table, she said, "New Great Idea." She bobbed her head like Major.

"I thought—" Esther turned to the other two as if for confirmation. "You said you weren't going to have Great Ideas anymore—"

"Because you kept getting into trouble," Vee finished, folding her arms across her chest and leaning back in the chair.

"But Major the reading mini was a Great Idea, and there was no trouble," Aneta put in with a nod that sent her ponytail bouncing.

Sunny waved her arms to dispel Vee and Esther's doubts. "It's okay to have a Great Idea as long as you finish." Pulling a fabric scrap from her pocket, Sunny dangled it in front of her friends. "This! I found *this* in the tractor shed. Even the sheriff missed it!"

The girls drew closer to inspect Sunny's prize. A triangular piece of material with rough edges, as though it had been torn from something bigger.

"Well?" Sunny watched Vee's face. If Vee, the only one who'd been close enough to the intruder, reacted as if fire ants were eating her toes, Sunny had been right and that scrap hadn't been in the shed for a bazillion years.

At first the dark-haired girl merely scrutinized the fabric. Then her eyes widened, and she gasped and lunged at the scrap. "The shirt— under the hoodie!"

"Exactly!" Sunny tossed the scrap onto the kitchen table where the girls regarded it as though it were a key to a treasure chest. She lowered her voice. "So that gave me an idea."

The other three leaned in.

This was more like it. Sunny stepped back and spun. Oh, it felt good to spin!

"Esther." She turned to the shorter girl who was folding and unfolding the fabric. Esther looked startled.

"What?"

"'Member Thursday, when you slept over—we felt creepy,

like someone was watching?"

The girl nodded.

"And the barn door was open a tiny bit?"

Aneta shivered. "That must have been so scary."

"Would have been a great time for the Anti-Trouble Phone," Vee remarked, straightening in her chair.

Sunny nodded.

Esther was still nodding, thinking. "Like someone was behind us or in the woods."

Pointing her finger at Esther, Sunny pronounced, "Exactly!"

Vee yawned. "Exactly what? My brain is tired. My mom will be here any minute."

Aneta placed her head on her hands, leaning on the table. "Hurry, Sunny. What is the great idea?"

Somewhat deflated, Sunny filled the girls in on her plan. She and Esther had felt creeped out with the unseen watcher in the woods.

"Check," Vee said, still yawning.

The intruder had run toward the meadow behind the corral, which was the same general direction.

"So?" Esther said.

"So, then, what if *we* started hunting for the guy *there*?"

"You mean, you think he's hanging around somewhere out in the woods?" Vee looked skeptical, but at least she leaned forward, an intent look on her tanned face.

This time it was Esther who shivered. "That is even more creepy."

"Have we ever heard a car driving away?" Sunny prodded. For pizza sake, they were hard to convince.

"Well, no." A shake of Aneta's head.

"Exactly!" Sunny loved playing detective.

Vee sighed and looked at the clock. "Exactly *what*, Sunny?"

"Then, wouldn't that mean he is somewhere *close*?"

"Oh," the girls said, each expression showing they finally got it. Aneta looked horrified, Vee slitted her eyes in the Vee Stare, and Esther chewed the inside of her cheek. Yup! The S.A.V.E. Squad girls were in the game.

"How are we going to find him in all the trees?"

"On horseback."

A chorus of three voices said, "Horseback?"

Then, "We haven't been out of the *corral* yet!"

Chapter 20

The Hunted Become the Hunters

$\mathcal{A}$s the girls had agreed, Sunny took lots of breaks the next day from reading her schoolwork to the animals and from unpacking final boxes in Uncle Dave's room. She talked loudly to herself and asked herself questions, as though someone was just out of sight.

They wanted The Shirt to stay away until. . .the hunt, which would begin after the girls arrived that afternoon and the Squad was at full power.

After the girls were dropped off, Sunny inspected the Squad. Esther wore her dad's camouflage sweatshirt, Aneta was in head-to-toe black with a straw cowboy hat, and Vee. . . Vee was wearing a *bright red jacket*. What was she thinking?

When Aneta's mom came for their riding lesson, the girls would show they were ready for a walk—Vee said to stress that they wanted to *walk*—in the meadow on horseback. Vee and Aneta would double ride Shirley, Esther would ride Mystery, and Sunny would ride Mondo.

Aneta's mother rubbed Shirley's big nose. "I heard from my mother that the library is delighted the zoo and the mini were such a hit. A reading mini. These big guys"—she slid the bit into the horse's mouth and looped the reins over the rail—"could no way go into the library or a school. Kind of makes him unique, doesn't it?"

Sunny's heart thumped happily. *Like me.*

"We were thinking. . ." Aneta spoke quietly as she saddled the patient Shirley. "Could we take the horses out of the corral today?"

"Ride them at a walk, of course," Vee said.

"Wearing helmets as usual," Esther added, tightening the cinch on Mystery.

The S.A.V.E. Squad was the rocko-socko, *no-doubt-about-it* best friends any girl on the planet could have. Sunny smiled hopefully at Ms. Jasper. What else was there to do? The girls had done it all!

Ms. Jasper cocked her head. "You four have done a great job with the horses. I like your seats—"

A snicker escaped Sunny. She knew Ms. Jasper was talking about how they sat on the horse, sitting up tall and holding in their stomachs, but still. *I mean, "seats" is just funny.*

Please, please, please.

Slowly, Ms. Jasper nodded. "I do think it's time for the next step."

"Yayness!" Sunny spun for joy.

"This is not exactly what I had in mind." Sunny stumbled over yet another rock in the meadow. Her sneakers were not made for this stuff. As she switched the reins to her left hand and patted Mondo with her right, she tossed back, "Thanks, Vee. *Walk* the horses?"

"Yeah, not what we thought at all," Esther agreed, puffing a little as she led Mystery.

"Hey, don't blame me. At least we're still getting to check the meadow and the woods near it." Vee nimbly leaped to the side as Shirley nearly tromped on her shoe.

Only Aneta remained unruffled, judging from the hilarity coming from the end of the line. Yes, Ms. Jasper said they could *walk* the horses. As in *not on* the horses. Sheesh. Sunny turned to see why Aneta wasn't minding that they weren't riding. She, of all of them, had taken to riding with great passion.

Behind Aneta trotted and waddled the zoo in their customary zigzag fashion. First Major with his head nodding, then Bob chewing a stick, Which Way alternately flapping his wings and waddling, and then—way back, Piggles. Who, Sunny noted, had just found a dirt hole and was sending up clouds of dust.

At first glance, she began to laugh, then her face turned serious. No sneaking up on the bad guy now. She brightened. But they *might* find more evidence that he was around and then tell Sheriff Bucholtz.

Esther and Vee had seen the parade behind them.

"Only we would do it this way!" Vee said.

Esther was shaking her head. "I don't think the cowboys in the movies did it this way, did they, Sunny?"

They continued leading their parade along the edge of the woods with this pattern: One Squader would hold the other's horse. That girl would plunge into the woods to see what she could see. So far, no one saw anything. The light was fading. Soon Aneta's mother would be looking for them. There had to be *something* from The Shirt somewhere nearby.

Esther had remembered to bring water bottles, and after a while they stopped, drank the water, and discussed what to do.

"I know my mom would not want us out much later." Aneta

looked at each girl through the dimming twilight.

"We don't want to kill our chances of maybe actually *riding* horses at a *walk* tomorrow," Esther added.

"Five more minutes," Sunny pleaded, picking up Mondo's reins and moving forward. "Just five more minutes."

"Not me," Esther said, her free hand going to her hip. "My feet are dead tired. Go ahead. I'll wait here."

Aneta chose to wait with Esther and play with the zoo, so Vee and Sunny handed over their reins and started a slow jog.

"For pizza sake, if you wanted to burgle a place," Sunny said, her hair flopping with each step, "wouldn't you want to be close by?"

Vee, who wasn't the slightest bit out of breath and seemed to know just where the dips and tripping points were, agreed. "I think we need to go deeper into the woods."

Sunny grinned. "That is a Great Idea, Vee. See, it's catching!"

The two eased into the shading trees at the edge of the meadow. The light dimmed dramatically. No more a pleasant meadow to run through and laugh in. Now? A Deep Dark Forest with all the fairy-tale scariness.

"Um," Sunny said, stopping.

Vee, behind, ran into her. "Yeah, like a different planet."

Looking back at the brighter light at the edge of the trees, Sunny said, "Okay, we have to go in a straight line or we'll get lost. Some city slicker in my uncle's movies didn't do that and the whole posse had to find them. It was dumb."

"Got it." Vee took off the red jacket. She dashed back to the edge of the woods and tied it to a tree branch. While backing her way to Sunny, she made sure she was in a straight line with the jacket.

"Vee," Sunny said as they resumed their foray into the woods. "If we die in here, I want you to know that you are the smartest girl I've ever known."

Two short minutes later, Vee was in the lead. She halted, and Sunny—looking back over her shoulder to make sure (a) they were still walking in a straight line and (b) no woods monsters were stalking them—promptly banged into her. Vee hit the ground and rolled to a sitting position, rubbing her hip. "Ow."

Sunny apologized and pulled her to her feet. "Why did you do that?"

Vee sniffed. "Smell."

Sunny wrinkled her face to drag in a deep breath of cooling wood air. Pines, dirt, and—

"Old fire!"

"Like you say, '*Exactly!*' "

"Spy mode!" Sunny whispered.

They crouched and began to walk like monkeys, low to the ground, on all fours in the direction of what they thought was the strongest smoke smell. Sunny, who had camped a lot with her family and at Bible camp, knew the difference between the fresh *I'm-burning-now* kind of fire and the old stomped-out kind of smell. This was stomped-out smoke.

Right about when Sunny thought her legs would curl up in knots and drop her into the dirt, she smelled the strongest smell yet.

"There." Vee sat down in the dirt and pointed. "There's The Shirt's camp."

Chapter 21

Something about That Wagon

*A*neta gave a little bounce. "Tell us again how you found this clue. It is very exciting."

The girls had managed to keep their wild fluttering under control enough to unsaddle the horses under Ms. Jasper's supervision, brush them down, turn them loose in the corral, and bring out hay.

After telling the girls they'd done well and that "you must have had a great time out there. You're all smiling. . . ," she said, "Aneta, I'm going to talk to Sunny's uncle for a bit. Then we'll load the Squad, minus Sunny, and head home."

Sunny watched Aneta's mother walk toward the house from where the girls sat in the barn. "She seems to like talking to my uncle," she observed.

Aneta smiled. "She said he was the smartest cowboy she's ever met. I guess she has met some stupid ones. That is sad because I like cowboys." She settled her straw cowboy hat more firmly on her head and pretended to pull two six-shooters from a belt.

"Hmm. . ." Vee's and Sunny's eyes met. They both glanced at Aneta, who had dropped the cowboy pose and hoisted herself up on two stacked bales of hay. She was ready for "all the deets" as Esther said. Vee shook her head just a tiny bit, and Sunny nodded in agreement. Not today. Aneta didn't need any more "deets" about anything other than the second clue.

Major blew a gusty sigh, folding his legs under him next to Sunny, who sat on the floor next to Aneta. Her heart soared. How cool it would be to have Major at her house. She would teach him to go potty outside. He could sleep in her room. She would walk him to the library for the Adventure Readers. He might become famous. She might become famous.

"Okay, let's have it one more time." Esther settled herself on the floor. "I still can't believe you touched the guy's stuff. That is so. . ." She fished for the word. "So ewww. I can't find a word for it."

Vee found her spot on top of another bale of straw ready to be spread in the stalls tomorrow. "It's not like there was an entire closet there and I touched his underwear—"

"EWW!" the girls shouted in unison.

Vee continued, but her rare smile tugged at the corner of her mouth. "It was a burned-out fire pit that was our final clue to his hideout."

Sunny threw back her head and flung her arms around Major. "You know that smell. The stomped-out fire smell. Not the *I'm-burning-now* fire smell."

Esther nodded while Aneta looked perplexed.

"Never mind, Aneta." Sunny grinned at her friend. "I just smelled the fire, and we started to follow the smell."

Aneta shivered. "You two were so brave. I think I might have run away."

"Ha!" Vee pointed a finger at Aneta and looked stern. "You're one of the bravest people I know. Stop saying that. Remember all the times you were brave for Wink?"

Esther stroked Which Way. Sunny didn't think a goose would be nearly as cool a pet as Major. Would they find a forever home for Which Way? Especially since the orange-beaked fowl created a never-ending supply of goose poo that Sunny had to hose off the barn floor and ramp daily. It was slippery stuff.

Forever homes.

Major leaving her.

Ughness.

She made herself concentrate on the latest clue.

Esther said, "We've got to go over this before Aneta's mother comes back and we all have to go." She grimaced. "I wish we didn't have to leave."

Sunny picked up the tale. "Right. We saw a camouflage tent. He thought he was being clever by sticking it under the big bushes. And it was there we found"—dramatic pause—"the clue!"

Vee added, "Sticking out of the tent!"

Sunny jumped in. "Only a part. Guess what part?" They all knew what part, but it was so fun to shout it again. Her Great Idea to keep on *just five minutes more* had worked. She'd followed through with it and look what had happened.

"The part where the fabric was ripped off!" Four voices shouted loudly enough that Which Way flapped into the air, Piggles snorted, Bob reared up, and Major stood and shook.

While they were still chortling at their cleverness and calming down the zoo, Sunny held up a hand. "The question now is—what's our next Great Idea?"

"Tell the police. Show them the fabric. Take them to the camp." Esther ticked off her ideas, one finger at a time. "End of story. The Squad saves the day!"

Vee shook her head. "There's more to it than that."

Esther stuck out her chin. "So what's *your* great plan?"

Vee took out her notebook and tiny pen from her back pocket. She began to write. Esther rolled her eyes. Would there ever be an adventure where Vee and Esther didn't butt heads at least once? The trouble was, they both thought they had the best ideas. Sunny swallowed a smile and a snort that almost—almost—popped out. *She* was the one with the *Great* Ideas.

"Okay, I just had to write some things down to help my brain," Vee said, glancing up from her notebook. "Here's the thing. Why was The Shirt in the barn at all? What's the difference between trashing the barn the second time and doing nothing the first time?"

Silence.

"Oh." Aneta furrowed her brow. "I see. What's different? That will be what he is really after."

"And he wouldn't tell the police if we turn him over now." Sunny began to nod. It wasn't a Great Idea yet, but it did sound like adventure. She looked over at Esther. Would their friend jump on board with their thinking, or would she stubbornly stick to her own idea?

She decided to try what her dad did with her sometimes. He asked what she thought he and Mom should do when he already knew. That way she thought it was her idea and would be more willing to go along. Sunny was pretty sure her dad didn't know she was onto him. It was a fun game. Most of the time. Except when she suggested they give the brothers away rather than come up with ideas on how to keep them out of her room. To Esther, she said, "So the guy gets away with—what? Murder?"

"Murder!" Aneta gasped. "Oh, Sunny." She stood up on the bale, looking around like she expected a corpse to suddenly appear. "Was he in the barn hiding a dead body?"

"No." Esther snapped her fingers and straightened. Which Way muttered and waddled off her lap to go lie next to Bob. "He was looking for something. The animals were the same. The hay and straw are the same. The. . ." She turned slowly and took stock of what was in the barn. "The saddles are the same, the bridles and the reins, all that horse stuff is the same. So what. . ." Her voice faded. She spread out her hands in inquiry.

Aneta said, "What is different?"

What was? Another scan of the barn's floor unleashed a rush of knowing. Sunny had to spin. Of course!

The girls waited.

"It's the *wagon*, guys. I moved it from the barn to the tractor shed because I was tired of tripping over it."

Two beats of each heart and then a flurry of running feet as the girls dashed toward the tractor shed. The zoo followed, nickering, grunting, flapping, and "bahhhhhbbb"-ing. The wagon remained where Sunny had placed it.

"Okay." Vee whipped out her notebook and pen. "Tell me what you see, and I'll write it down."

"Four old wheels, two poles for Major to get in between." If Esther hadn't been quickly scanning the wagon while she spoke, Sunny knew Vee's eyes would have narrowed, thinking that Esther was making fun of her and her notebook. But Esther was absorbed in looking at *all* the details of the wagon. Vee started to write.

Aneta ran her fingers over the uneven, weathered sides of the small wagon. "This is so the kid can't fall out. It would have to be a very small kid. Nothing I see here." She ran her fingers over the glued-down piece of old carpet. "And an icky old piece of carpet for them to sit on." She crinkled her nose. "That carnival man was not clean."

Thumping back down to the floor, Sunny planted her elbows on her knees and then her head on her hands. She squinted. What was so amazingly important about this wagon? Vee wrote down everything Aneta and Esther continued to report while Sunny kept thinking. Who was The Shirt? What did he want with the wagon?

"Okay, I have the answer." Vee made one last note and climbed into the John Deere seat. "Ready for the report?"

The girls nodded. Esther wiped her hands on the back of her capris and joined Sunny on the floor. Aneta sat sideways on the old saddle nearby.

Vee cleared her throat. "It's a wagon." She made a face. "That's all it is."

Groans greeted her announcement. Vee smiled a tiny smile. "Sorry, there was nothing really to tell so I thought I better make it sound sort of interesting."

After that, nobody spoke for several minutes. The shed was dark enough Sunny could barely make out the faces she knew so well. Thinking. They were all thinking. "I guess we need to write down everything since the first time we saw the wagon," Sunny said with a sigh. "Who knows how long we've got until Aneta's mom hauls you guys away."

It was better, though, that Uncle Dave talk to Aneta's mom than be on the phone to those sport pony people. "I wish my uncle would do secondhand horses." She drifted off for a moment, imagining her uncle's ranch with happy horses and happy people adopting happy horses or coming to see them and learning how to care kindly for happy horses.

"And—earth to Sunny," Esther raised her voice.

"Oh." Sunny came back to earth. "Just thinking about how cool it would be for my uncle to have a secondhand horse ranch rather than sport ponies for Arab sheiks."

"Sunny's right. We need a list," Vee agreed. Aneta shrugged and said okay. Esther sighed, but nodded.

"I'm ready," Vee said, pen poised over the notebook.

After much back and forth and a teeny bit of arguing between Vee and Esther about what was important enough to go on the list, the girls came up with this:

The carnival—the wagon was inside the little enclosure in the corral where the creepy guy stood.
The wagon was the first thing the creepy carnival guy took out of the front seat of the truck when he delivered the zoo.
He said Major really liked it and to keep it close to him.
It was the last thing he talked about before he left in a hurry.

"I remember now." Sunny snapped her fingers. She'd been the one to provide the last two items on Vee's list. "I thought it was kind of cute that Major liked his wagon."

Sliding off the saddle and standing up, Aneta brushed off the back of her black leggings and frowned. "But Major does not care about the wagon. You put the wagon in the tractor shed, and he does not care."

Esther nodded. "Yeah. Anyone think they've seen him looking for it?"

Vee snorted. "He's only looking for those baby carrots you give him, Sunny."

The grating of gravel.

"Girls? Time to go."

"Aneta's mom," Vee said. "Everybody keep thinking about the wagon. It's *got* to have something to do with that wagon."

Chapter 22

Clue #3 Shows Up

"Sunny, don't think that this lovely afternoon snack of pretzels and hummus is going to change my mind. I'm done adding secondhand horses. It's sport ponies for me now."

Today, for the first time since his accident, Uncle Dave looked like himself. The brown puddles of pain were no longer hanging under his eyes. He stood straight on the crutches, and he'd eaten her very wonderful homemade hummus at the kitchen table with her. All wonderful. What was not so wonderful was his insistence that finding more secondhand horses would not be a good thing for the ranch.

Sunny ordered her face to look pitiful. "So many horses already living and needing homes. Why make more?"

He raised his eyebrows over his coffee cup, took a sip, and made an ugly face. "Where did you read that argument, my favorite niece?" He set the cup down. "I need to teach you how to make coffee. Are you done with school?"

"Yep. And all the animals are fine. Major likes history better than science. Me, too, except the Middle Ages are kind of gross and dirty." She'd read out loud as she worked through her assignments. School was so much more fun with a miniature horse breathing down your neck. "The Squad will be here soon." This weekend while they were all at the ranch, they had to figure out *why* The Shirt wanted the wagon.

Which Way sounded the "incoming" alarm seconds before Sunny heard the gravel. "That's them!" Once through the front door and the screen, Sunny squinted at what was *not* one of the parents' vehicles. Standing next to an old truck that looked like it had gotten a thorough washing was a tall man and a teenage boy. A horse trailer was hitched, and inside it Sunny heard the stomps of a hoof and saw a horse's face through the open window.

Was this the first sport pony and her uncle had not told her? She walked over to the trailer and stuck out her hand like she'd seen Uncle Dave do. "Are you the guy with the sport pony?"

The man reached out his own hand, rough and scratchy, and clasped Sunny's firmly. It felt, like Uncle Dave often said, "like he worked hard for a living." "Don't know about no sport pony, but I've got a great cutting horse in there." His voice roughened; he cleared his throat.

"What's a cutting horse?"

Another vehicle pulled in. Esther's dad deposited Vee, Esther, and Aneta and drove off.

The three dashed over to stand by Sunny, their normal greeting extinguished by the unexpected visitors.

"He has a cutting horse," Sunny volunteered to her friends.

The tall boy next to him didn't say a word, but Sunny was sure he wasn't blinking hard to keep the dust out of his eyes. The wind wasn't blowing yet. Was he *crying*?

The front door shrieked and popped. There was another stomp in the trailer. The boy stepped up on the wheel and spoke some low words. Uncle Dave stood on the porch, crutches under each arm.

"That your father?" the man asked Sunny.

She shook her head. "Uncle. We're helping out here on the ranch until his ankle gets better."

He gestured to the rest of the Squad. "Sisters?"

"Best friends," Aneta said as Uncle Dave joined them. "Mr. Martin, this man has a cutting horse. What do you have that a horse needs to cut?" Her face revealed her curiosity.

The boy snorted. "You girls don't know horses, do you?"

Sunny smothered the immediate grin that wanted to march across her face. That was going to fire up Vee and Esther. Esther had done a lot of Internet research on horses, geese, pygmy goats, and pigs that helped them on the ranch. Vee wrote everything down they had learned so they wouldn't forget it for the next time.

"No, nothing." Vee crossed her arms over her chest and widened her stance in the gravel. "Just that they have four legs."

"A tail," Esther added, her fists flying to her hips.

"And need to be saddled with the cinch tight. Some horses bloat on purpose so the saddle gets loose and you fall off," Aneta said.

The other three girls' eyebrows rose in perfect sync.

When did Aneta learn all that cowboy talk?

The boy's eyes narrowed then he smiled. "Okay. I was a jerk. Sorry."

"Is this horse yours?" Aneta asked.

The smile vanished. "Yeah." He clamped his lips and strode off behind the back of the trailer.

The man asked if he could speak with Uncle Dave privately, so the girls retreated to the porch railing. Since they couldn't see the boy, they began guessing what the man wanted.

"The man wants to sell the horse. Betcha." Esther pushed hair out of her eyes as the wind picked up. "Did anyone figure out why the bad guy wants the wagon?"

"What is a cutting horse anyway?" Vee asked, turning to Esther. "And no, I didn't. Did either of you?"

Esther promptly replied, "A cutting horse is used to cut cattle from the herd. I read on the Internet that a well-trained cutting horse can practically work by himself once he knows what's going on."

"No ideas on the wagon." Sunny shook her head. So did Aneta. "Uncle Dave is shaking his head and pointing to the corral. I'm thinking he doesn't want to buy the horse." Sunny listened as hard as she could, but she could only hear the wind and the deep voices.

Shirley, Mondo, Mystery, and Major came to their corral railings to watch. Finally, Uncle Dave threw up his hands and nodded. The man stuck out his hand. The two men shook hands, after which the man called the boy. He reappeared, his shoulders bowed. He'd tipped his hat way down so you couldn't see his eyes.

"Wow. He doesn't want to hear what he's going to hear," Vee observed.

Sunny agreed. Little swirls of dust rose from his shuffling boots. The father—Sunny figured it was father and son since they had the same skinny nose and cheekbones—pointed to her uncle and spoke. At first the boy's shoulders hunched as though he were expecting a blow. Then his head snapped up.

"That wasn't what he thought was going to happen!" Esther bounced on the railing. "I wish we could hear what's going on!"

"He is happy now. He is shaking your uncle's hand, Sunny," Aneta said.

The girls streamed over to the boy once Sunny's uncle and the boy's dad moved off toward the corral.

"Your uncle is the best," the boy said, his face no longer tight with tears. He had bright blue eyes that were sparkling. "He said he would take care of my horse for free until my dad gets a new job and gets caught up with bills. He said I can come work with my horse anytime. I can't come every day because I work and go to school, but I'll be here whenever I can."

Sunny's insides glowed with pride at her uncle. Another second-hand horse. Maybe Uncle Dave didn't realize it yet, but he really was a secondhand horse rancher. Sport ponies? She didn't think so.

"Since you girls can ride Starbright while he's here, let me show you something cool about the saddle, even though you'll use a different one to ride regular." The boy opened the tack area of the trailer and hauled out the prettiest saddle Sunny had ever seen. Under the seat part, leather rectangles stacked on leather rectangles. Every inch of the rectangles had carvings on them. Some were light; some were dark.

"Um." Sunny looked at the other girls who were staring at the horse in the trailer. The horse blinked out his window. Sunny would bet Major could walk under his belly if the little mini lowered his head. "We're still beginning riders. Starbright is a pro cutting horse and all."

"Ah, he's a sweetie with beginners. He knows they don't know anything. Check out this saddle."

The girls oohed and ahhed; the boy seemed to appreciate that.

"Here's the cool part." He lifted a flap of leather that had tiny stars carved into it. "For Starbright," the boy said proudly. "When we won the Junior Cutting championship last year, I was the youngest and so was he."

He gave them a quick overview of why a cutting saddle was built the way it was. Sunny wasn't paying much attention. Her eyes were glued to the leather flap the boy had lifted up. Underneath the flap was a matching set of twinkle stars carved in the leather. At first glance, it looked like just a fancy underside. But Sunny's scrutiny caught the slightly thicker edge. As the boy continued to instruct the other three—who were hanging on his every word—Sunny reached forward and slid her finger along the thicker edge. Her finger disappeared into a secret compartment.

A secret compartment! Zip, zip, zip went her brain. She glanced toward the tractor shed. Clue number three had finally shown up.

"So you found the secret." The boy interrupted his lecture to smile at Sunny. He did have a nice smile, but it didn't make Sunny blush. In fact, she wasn't sure she heard anything else the boy said after he stated, "Looks just like a normal saddle, doesn't it?"

She whirled to face the Squad. "Just a normal saddle? Like maybe just a normal *wagon*?"After a quick dance in the dust and a spin, she took off for the barn, throwing the last words over her shoulder. "We'll take good care of your horse. Thank you for coming!"

Oh, the hunted were after the hunter again.

This time for keeps.

In the length of time it took the girls to finish talking to the boy and he and his father to drive off, she had reached the barn, had the wagon on its side, and was running her hands over it.

"Sunny, what are you talking about?" Aneta asked. "What are you doing?"

Esther collapsed to her knees on the opposite end of the wagon from where Sunny was rapping with her knuckles on the end. "I get it. There's a secret compartment in this wagon."

"Somewhere." Vee knelt on one of the long sides and began sliding her fingers. "This time tap and see if anything sounds hollow."

Aneta nodded and sat cross-legged across from Vee. She began to tap, bending close to the wagon to listen.

Sunny had tapped, pounded, and fingered every bit of her end. "Nothing," she said in disgust, falling back on her elbows and regarding the wagon.

"This gross carpet has got to come off." Esther made a face. "It's the only place we haven't been able to listen for a hollow sound."

"Then off it comes." Sunny straightened up and began to tug at her end. With all four pulling, and comments about how dirty it was, the carpet came off. Some bits stuck, but now the girls could see the five boards.

"I see it!" Aneta shouted, using her index finger to trace a slightly raised board. She pushed long and hard on it. Nothing happened.

"Let me." Sunny reached over. She took her fist and pounded. Nothing.

Vee rapped on it with her knuckles. A satisfying hollow sound made the girls' eyes go large and round. "It really *is* a secret compartment," Vee breathed, with a full, satisfied smile.

Now they all looked at Esther. What would she try to open this tantalizing compartment? Esther studied the wagon boards. Then she suddenly leaned forward and, using her fingertips, pressed down quickly and let up.

The slat popped up about a quarter of an inch.

"But I did that," Aneta protested.

"Nope," Esther said. "You pushed and held. Sunny punched it. It's a light touch and then hands off. My mom has a jewelry box that opens that way." Four sets of hands eagerly pulled up the board the rest of the way. When the compartment lay fully exposed, an "ooooo!" rolled through the shed.

A black velvet bag lay on the rough wood.

Chapter 23

A Bag of Bones?

"Well, don't just stare at it, pick it up and open it," Esther said, staring at it and not picking it up.

"You pick it up," Vee retorted with a snort. She sat on her hands. "I—well, I guess I didn't think we'd actually *find* anything."

"What's in it?" Aneta clasped her hands in front of her and sat back with a mild thump.

"It's treasure, that's what it is. I know it!" Sunny reached over and picked up the bag, her fingers trembling. The velvet felt thick, warm, and soft to her exploratory fingers. At the bottom, a faint bulge pushed out the fabric. She squeezed the bulge between thumb and fingers. "It's like—crunchy."

"Bones?" Aneta's eyes widened, and she scuttled backward. "Maybe the man *did* murder someone."

Esther shook her head matter-of-factly. "Too small of a bag."

Vee plopped next to Sunny and spread out an ancient burlap feed bag on the wagon bottom. "Found this. I shook out all the loose stuff, whatever it all was. I didn't want to look too close."

Sunny poured the contents of the velvet bag out onto the rough burlap. The last bits of sparkle lay on the burlap, catching the afternoon light from the gaps in the roof.

Vee looked at Esther.

Esther looked at Aneta.

Aneta looked at Sunny.

Glowing red rubies, deep green emeralds, glittering diamonds. Sunny could not think of a thing to say. She couldn't even spin.

"*Now* we call the police," Esther said, her hands going to her hips in a don't-mess-with-me attitude.

"Are they real?" asked Vee, ever doubting.

"*Just* like in the girl detective books," Aneta breathed, her face shining with excitement.

Sunny was up and spinning around the tractor shed, keeping an eye out for potential tripping obstacles. When dizziness careened her into the John Deere, she put her hands out and pushed off from it, standing with her legs wide.

"What is it?" Vee wanted to know.

"Another Great Idea?" Aneta asked hopefully, poking her finger among the jewels on the burlap.

"Somehow I already know. I. Don't. Like. It." Esther was already frowning.

"Not a *Great* Idea." Sunny shook her head at Esther then squatted near the wagon, staring in awe. "Only the Greatest Idea that *ever* showed up on the planet."

A few minutes later, Esther continued to not like the Greatest Idea, even after Sunny explained in detail how it involved the girls, Bob, and a trampoline. "We should tell your uncle and have him call the police."

"But the police would be happier if they caught the bad guy *and* the jewels, wouldn't they?" Aneta looked around the group for confirmation.

"We're helping them," Vee agreed. She had written down everything Sunny said. Now she reviewed it. "It's a crazy idea, but it actually might work. You heard how nutso the guy was when he ran screaming from the barn last time." She poked her finger through the deep glowing red, green, and white stones. "Where do you think he stole these from?"

"If I—I mean, we—catch the bad guy and return the jewels,"— she needed to say the right words here—"then my Uncle Dave and my parents will see that I can finish something. And finish something rocko-socko *giant!*"

Esther chewed her lip while she regarded the glittering bits on the burlap. When she looked up, her eyes looked bright, like there were tears in them. "I'll do it. For you."

A quick hug for Esther and another spin. This really *was* what she was good at. Even in her biggest wonders, she'd never dreamed she'd be getting a Great Idea to catch a criminal.

"Except I don't see why Vee doesn't get Bob. She runs faster," Aneta stated.

"That's what I was thinking. No offense, Aneta." Vee tipped her head inquiringly at Sunny. "I'm just faster on land. Aneta's faster in water."

Nodding, Sunny said, "Yeah, I know. Think about it, guys. Who is Bob going to follow the fastest?"

Aneta and Vee shared a look.

"Aneta!" Vee said.

"Me!" Aneta said.

Sunny flung her arms wide. "Did I not think of *everything?*"

"So it's tonight we set the trap." Esther smacked one fist into the other.

"Catch a bad man," Aneta said.

"Return the jewels to the rightful owner." Vee stood and brushed off her pants.

"Be heroes," Sunny said. *And show everyone I can finish big stuff.* Maybe after this she'd be a detective. She could make up business cards: SUNNY'S DETECTIVE AGENCY.

"Sunny!"

"Huh? What?"

"We're going in for supper now," Esther said, choking a little on her chuckle.

The girls trooped into the house where Ms. Jasper and Uncle Dave were sitting at the kitchen table eating peanut butter cookies.

Aneta's mom looked more beautiful than ever. She was laughing at something Uncle Dave had said—Sunny knew it had to be pretty funny—with her head thrown back and her long blond hair cascading down her back. Hmmm. She wasn't wearing it in the ponytail or the hair clip like she usually did when she was a lawyer.

"Hi, girls." She turned to smile at them. Aneta came up to her and slid an arm around her mother's shoulder. "Hi, sweetie." She hugged her daughter sideways. "I ordered pizza for all of us so nobody has to cook. Not that you, Sunny, haven't been taking stellar care of your uncle!" She turned her smile on Sunny.

Pizza? Pizza was terrible news.

"You are staying for dinner?" Aneta asked, her brow furrowing. Her mom, who had responded to a question from Uncle Dave, gave her a nod and another hug and went back to talking with Uncle Dave about how they might help the guy who needed a job so he could take his son's cutting horse back home.

"That's—um, great," Esther said from her place next to Uncle Dave, but her voice didn't sound like it was great. She looked over at Sunny.

Vee looked like someone had slapped her. Her mouth opened and closed, minus words.

Sunny reviewed the options while conversation about Starbright swirled around her.

They could quit.

Nope. That wasn't an option.

They could—she was thinking wildly now—start a fight among the four of them and break up dinner together.

No. Bad idea. Then everyone would go home. Or the adults would make them discuss the issue and take even more time.

She could insist they cancel pizza because what the Squad really wanted was peanut butter and jelly sandwiches and to go to bed early.

Yeah. Like Uncle Dave and Aneta's mom would believe *that*.

How late would Aneta's mother stay? What if she came out to the barn and asked questions while they were setting up the trap? A shiver zinged down Sunny's spine. She tuned in to the conversation, the special—*friendly*—tones her uncle and Ms. Jasper used with each other.

When her Greatest Idea had first come to her, she planned it would be done tonight. Uncle Dave and her family would have proof that Sunny was good for something and could finish. Could they get Aneta's mom to leave early? Sunny didn't see any way to do that. Uncle Dave was already talking about the John Wayne movie he wanted Aneta's mom to watch with him.

Great. That meant there was only one thing to do. The Squad would have to set the trap after Ms. Jasper went home. The best they could hope for was no conversation after the movie ended.

But what if The Shirt came to the barn for the wagon—and what he thought was still *in* the wagon—while everyone was chomping down pizza?

Chapter 24

Setting the Trap

Shhh!"

"Be quiet."

Clunk!

"Be careful, you guys." Sunny pulled off her sweatshirt and placed it under the wheels of the wagon so it muffled the sounds of it going through the bedroom window.

"Okay." Vee stood inside the bedroom. "I've got the front."

"I'm glad Esther figured out how to remove the poles," Aneta said from her position next to Sunny outside. The two girls lifted up the back wheels, spitting at the dislodged dust and dirt. "We have to finish before the pizza guy gets here."

"I hope that's dirt we're spitting out," Sunny said.

Aneta's face contorted into a *total ick* expression. "Oh, Sunny."

Through the closed door of the bedroom, Sunny heard Uncle Dave's maniacal laugh and Ms. Jasper's softer, full-throated chuckle. "For pizza sake, what can be so *funny* all the time?"

"Be glad," Esther said. "At least they won't hear us clunking and banging." She and Vee leaned out of the window to guide in the back end of the wagon. "There!"

Once Vee had rolled the wagon to the other side of the room, Aneta and Sunny each jumped up, dove in headfirst, and rolled to standing. The girls returned to the living room to, as Vee said, "establish their alibis."

Forever.

That's how long it seemed to the girls for Aneta's mom to leave.

They ate pizza.

They watched the cowboy movie.

The zoo stomped on the front porch halfway through. The girls had to return them to the barn, closing the door securely.

"As soon as I get around on these crutches, I've got to find out how they escape from the corrals," Uncle Dave said. "I've never had animals so nosy."

Did that mean her uncle was thinking the zoo might *stay*?

No sign of The Shirt as the girls led the zoo back to the barn.

"But how would you know if he *was* around?" Aneta whispered into Sunny's ear on the return trip to the house.

"I would feel his creepiness," Sunny whispered back. *Do not look over your shoulder.* She hoped The Shirt would show up tonight, get caught, and finish her Greatest Idea.

Aneta shivered and ran for the front door.

Finally, after ten, as the girls yawned jaw-cracking yawns and talked about how tired they were, Aneta's mom kissed her daughter good night, said good-bye to the other three and to Uncle Dave—that took a little longer—and left.

Vee and Sunny shared another look. Esther grinned knowingly.

Aneta looked at the three. "What is funny?"

"Adults are weird," Sunny said, linking her arm with her blond, taller friend and walking toward the girls' bedroom. "And *they* think *eleven*-year-olds are weird."

They made noise going back and forth to the hall bathroom, chattering about good tooth hygiene and smothering honks of laughter. Shortly after that, Uncle Dave called good night. Soon the house was dark.

But not quiet and still. At least not in the girls' bedroom.

Sunny threw herself on the bed. "I can't believe I just ate pizza with millions of dollars of jewels in my cargo capri leg pocket."

"We are nuts," Vee said. "Your Great Idea—"

"Greatest," Sunny interrupted.

"—is borderline insane."

"Borderline?" Esther pulled out the heavy, big-nosed flashlight from her backpack. "Please. We *are* insane." She gestured. "My dad's emergency flashlight. I figure this is an emergency."

Vee pulled out a tiny narrow one and shone it on the wall. Half the wall exploded into bright white light. "Bill gave me this after I cleaned his garage. I told him he should have given it to me before. I could have found stuff easier. He's a pack rat."

"What are you doing, Sunny?" Aneta asked, looking over at Sunny who was rummaging through the drawers of the small dresser.

"Looking for something dark to wear so when we hide, The Shirt won't see us. There!" With a triumphant yip, she pulled a dark navy hoodie out of the bottom drawer. Pulling it over her head, she spoke through the material. "Now, everyone knows what they're supposed to do?"

The girls assured her they did, but Vee wanted to go through it again anyway, which made Esther frown and stick her hands on her hips, but Aneta made everything right by saying that it was okay because lots of times someone did that very thing in books.

"Not necessarily," Esther began then removed her fists from her hips and shrugged. Sunny breathed a sigh of relief. The last thing they needed right now was a bossy contest between Vee and Esther.

Vee and Aneta swung their legs out the window, dropped the distance to the ground, and held up their arms for the wagon. Sunny and Esther grunted a little—it was so awkward to hold it up—but this time managed to without banging the house and waking up Uncle Dave—or the zoo. *So far: yayness one, ughness zero.*

Vee did a quick check-dash around the corner to make sure Uncle Dave's light was off and the window closed, reported they were, and the foursome, each holding some part of the wagon off the ground, tiptoed along the driveway.

"Sunny, you're scuffing your feet! You'll wake up your uncle." Esther's supposed-to-be-whisper boomed out like a cannon in the darkness.

"Shhh!" everyone said.

Esther's voice dropped to a growl. "Well, you are."

They arrived at the barn door, set down the wagon, and waited while Aneta opened the door. It didn't make a sound. Sunny patted herself on the back for oiling the hinges. Then she patted the pocket on the leg of her capris. The bag was still there. She was getting good at this following-through stuff. Just wait until Uncle Dave found out they had caught The Shirt *and* the stolen jewels. Sunny blinked furiously, trying to adjust her eyes as she pushed the door closed.

Vee and Esther had yet to flash their lights to illuminate the nearly pitch blackness of the shed.

Wait.

She sniffed.

What was that?

Dark air thickened around her, robbing her of her bearings. It stunk like. . .BO—big-time.

Where were the girls?

Where was the wagon?

She moved her foot ahead of her cautiously.

Something is wrong.

The creepy feeling that night with Esther slid over her like a wave at a wave park. "Hurry, Vee—Esther—turn on those flashlights!"

A split second before light revealed the familiar tractor shed, a rough voice grunted, "I've been waiting for you girls."

Chapter 25

Operation Shirt

Squinting in the flashlights, a man wearing a red-striped, long-sleeved shirt with the sleeves rolled up held a length of chain Sunny remembered putting in the WHO KNOWS? pile. A triangular patch of the shirt was missing.

"It is *you*?" Aneta said, disbelief stringing her voice out to a hoarse whisper.

"The Shirt!" Sunny said then attempted to hold her breath and talk. "Eww. You're still *wearing* it?"

"Not you!" Vee's mouth hung open.

"Creepy carnival guy!" Esther gasped. She backed toward the door behind them, but quicker than Sunny had seen Which Way capture a bug, The Shirt had sidestepped them and blocked their only exit. His grin of victory looked even more frightening in the glare of the flashlight.

The only way they could finish the Greatest Idea was if the other three girls got out of the shed. She had to get him away from the door.

"Get those flashlights outta my eyes! Gimme those!" he snarled. He started forward, fists clenched in the chain, toward Esther, who now stood motionless. "Gimme that, fat girl!"

For pizza sake, could he have said something *worse*?

Now that her own eyes had somewhat adjusted, Sunny saw Esther's eyes bug out. Her chest swelled. "Sure," Esther said, pulling back her arm. "Here's *mine*!" Emitting a scream that curled Sunny's hair tighter, she hurled a perfect hatchet throw, just like in the movies. The flashlight tumbled end over end toward The Shirt. With the light dipping and flipping in and out of his vision, his head waggled from side to side, trying to dodge the light and keep his eye on the girls. So when the top-heavy flashlight slammed into his throat, he was a bit unprepared.

"Gahhh!" he clutched his throat. "Gahhh!"

"And here's *mine*!" Vee ran four tiny steps forward in the semi-darkness, jerking her tiny ultrabright up and down. It flickered the light much like Esther's had. The Shirt was gagging and swinging the chain toward them. Sunny sidestepped one swing. Vee drew him away from the door. Aneta was edging behind The Shirt and nearly to the door latch.

It was time.

"Operation Shirt! Operation Shirt!" Sunny whooped. She clapped her hand on the side pocket, felt the bulky velvet bag, turned, and bolted toward the stairs.

"Hey!" The raspy choked voice didn't sound quite so smug. "Get back here. I know you got them jewels!"

"Catch me!" Sunny sang out, suddenly brave, her foot on the bottom rung of the stairs. The other three had vanished from the shed. The Shirt seemed undecided on whether to follow them or Sunny. Sunny dashed up the stairs, praying that the Greatest Idea would work.

A rumble grated a few steps behind her. She couldn't call it laughter. It was too evil. "Ha-ha, stupid kid, there's no way to get down from there."

He stumbled his way across the floor, knocking over an old milk can and wooden boxes. "I got you good. You been in my way since that crummy carnival."

Oh, dear Lord, I hope this is the Greatest Idea and that You gave it to me, 'cause if it isn't, that guy is really mad at me.

He was halfway up the steps, his breath wheezing in great gasps. "Gonna—get—*pant, pant*—you, stupid kid." That flashlight had to have hurt. Esther had some muscle behind that arm. But Sunny didn't feel sorry for him. He treated the zoo badly and stole jewels. Now he had called her stupid. Maybe he would fall down the stairs from a heart attack and she wouldn't have to do what she had to do.

Oh dear.

What if he did?

What would she do *then*?

She had reached the window where, it seemed like a year ago, she'd scared the Squad and caused Uncle Dave's accident. Looking down, she caught the glimmer of the silver edges of the tramp. She heard whispering, and she heard Bob.

Good.

The Shirt stopped two steps from the top, leaning over and blowing hard. He was probably two Uncle Dave–lengths away. "Ha-ha," he gasped. "Joke's on you." It took him another few breaths to continue. "You got nowhere to go. Gimme the bag and I won't slap you around too much."

Sunny felt an odd sort of power. He was so out of breath. What she was going to do in the next moment would be brilliant, and The Shirt would be toast. "It's wrong to steal, and you didn't treat the zoo very well. They don't like you."

Part of that power *whoosh* was exciting—the jump-off-the-swings-at-the-very-top exciting when your guts kind of flop up and hang there until the moment you plunge down. The feeling that followed wasn't so nice. She felt, well, yucky. Just because he called Esther fat and her stupid didn't mean she should be like him.

She was not stupid.

He would soon see that.

With a roar, he lunged for her in midgasp. Sunny screamed and for the second time sprang out the window.

Vee, Aneta, and Esther were holding the tramp's wobbly legs steady—from underneath. She couldn't resist her tramp pattern: *Bounce, bounce, drop, slap, clap!* and, she was off.

"Thanks, guys," she whispered. Bob the goat sounded like he was chewing. Aneta had done her part. Brought the goat and would keep him quiet until the right moment. Sunny stepped away from the tramp and looked up.

Above, The Shirt clung to the sides of the shed window. "Stupid! That's what you are. I'm gonna get a running start and land on you like a ton of bricks."

"Now," Sunny muttered out of the corner of her mouth.

Before he could disappear into the duskiness of the loft, the tramp began to move back and forth. And then an eerie voice began to bleat.

"Bahhhhhb! Bahhhhb!" Bob had run out of treats at just the right time.

"What?" The moon reflected off a sweaty face so contorted with fear he looked like a gargoyle out of a history book.

"Baahhhhhb!" said Bob. "Bahhhhhb!" The little goat was politely requesting more treats.

The tramp swayed back and forth in a wild dance. The Shirt jumped back as though at the next moment it would float up and bite him in the nose. Kind of funny in a scary sort of way, although Sunny wished he'd get moving so they could complete the next part. "C– can't be. There ain't no such things as ghosts. That tramp ain't really moving!" He yelled, backing away. A crash followed. Had he run into something? She smiled. The Squad had never found the time to clean that loft. Sometimes *not* finishing worked out.

Feet pounded down the wooden stairs.

"Now, Vee! Pour it on!" Sunny shouted.

Her speedy friend scrambled out from under the tramp and streaked around the corner. According to the Greatest Idea, Vee would get to the door and bolt it from the outside, effectively trapping The Shirt in until Uncle Dave called the sheriff. *Finished.* No way would he dare jump out the window onto the "haunted" tramp while Bob was there. Just why he was so afraid of Bob she didn't know, but it sure was a fun part of the idea.

A crash interrupted her thoughts of victory and how proud everyone would be of her. The Shirt must have tripped on the stairs. Aneta and Esther, who had crab-walked out from under the tramp as well with Bob the goat in tow, winced.

"I think he took the fast way down," Aneta said, shaking her head and petting Bob. "Good goat."

Near the front of the shed, Vee let out a "Whoa!" that morphed into a brittle cry of pain, a muffled shriek, and a thud.

The door to the shed banged.

Not banged closed and bolted.

Banged *open*.

Chapter 26

The Chase

With Bob bouncing behind, the three girls beat feeted it around the corner, along the side of the shed, and skidded to the front. Vee lay sprawled on the cement ramp in front of the shed door, struggling to get up.

The shed door was open.

No sign of the creepy carnival guy.

"What happened, Vee?" Aneta bent over her friend.

"Where *is* he?" Sunny asked, assisting Esther and Aneta with getting Vee upright. Their quickly moving friend had sailed into the stuff Sunny had been hosing since the zoo arrived. Goose droppings. Green, worse than anything you've ever smelled, and, as Vee found out—*slippery*.

"Don't touch me, I'm polluted!" she cried, pulling away from the helping hands. "That way. He's gone that way!" She pointed a green-smeared finger toward the side of the house. "Eww! I reek!"

He was running for his camp in the trees. Toward wherever he had stashed the truck and trailer. He'd escape, and they'd never get him and the jewels.

The jewels. She patted her pocket. They were still there. They had something. But Sunny wanted The Shirt, too. After all, he had been mean to the zoo.

"Horses!" Esther cried. "We'll get on the horses and catch him!"

Piggles, Major, and Which Way, somehow out of the barn again, milled around. Which Way was happily unconcerned he'd been the cause of a major kink in the Greatest Idea. Sunny darted toward the running man and then back, out and back again, indecisive. "Are you kidding? Do you remember how long it takes us to saddle up *one* horse?"

"No way." Vee's voice came from the shed. "We're way too slow. We'll have to catch him on foot."

Esther sighed. "We always end up running. Can't we ever do a computer search to catch the bad guy?"

Vee emerged, holding up two rusty objects. "Weapons." She jerked her head. "Go get yours."

"Right!" Aneta dashed into the dim interior. "I remember something."

Sunny and Esther were close behind. "Whoa!" Sunny stopped short; Esther ran into her.

"Oops," Esther said. "Remember. Blink a lot so you can see in the dark."

"I've got my weapon!" Sunny ran out.

Esther said, "I'll use yours, too, Aneta. Let's get out of here!" They charged out of the shed behind Sunny. The zoo wasn't sure what to make of all this yelling and dashing in and out and on the ground and up again, so they made their own noises and circled the girls, causing more confusion until Vee shouted.

"There he is!" She broke out of the melee and took off.

Sunny thought The Shirt would have gotten farther by now.

"Hey!" Esther shrieked in his direction, holding up the end of her weapon. "You better stop. We're armed and dangerous!"

He didn't stop.

"He's limping!" Aneta said. Sunny, behind Vee, shouted back, "Probably that fast way down the stairs!" She threw a look over her shoulder to see how Esther was doing.

"Esther! Aneta! Look at the zoo!"

Esther turned around. When she turned back, her frowning face had transformed into a bright smile. "They're so crazy."

Of course, the zoo was following them. First Major as usual, trotting along like a famous prize stallion—only bitty, his white mane floating. Sunny's heart swelled with love for him. He was so wonderful.

Bob was next, bleating, "Bahhhhhb!" That ought to freak out The Shirt if he heard it floating behind him. Which Way had hitched a ride on Piggles the Pig. Piggles had great ideas too, like being in on all the adventures, but his short legs only carried him until he found a dusty spot or someplace wet. They would have to look for him on the way back and not trip over him.

Still no lights or Uncle Dave's voice as she passed his window.

They must all look crazy, Sunny thought, staggering over the rough ground. The police should be here soon. Why didn't she hear sirens? Putting on a burst of speed, she came alongside Vee.

"Where's the police?"

Vee didn't look at her. She wasn't panting or looking like she was streaking along in the dark in a rough meadow. Sunny stumbled again, her right ankle twisting into a quick sear of pain. What if this Greatest Idea turned out to be terrible, like the others? What would Uncle Dave say? Her parents? It was hard to keep running on that ankle and keep up with Vee, but she did.

They were catching up. Aneta, Esther, and Bob joined Vee and

Sunny. Piggles had indeed stopped a while back. Which Way was flapping and waddling onward. Another couple of minutes and the Squad would take The Shirt down. In the movies, someone always said, "We're gonna take him down."

"Vee! We're gonna catch up with him, like right now! The police aren't here. Didn't you call them?"

"No." Vee said it so quietly at first Sunny wasn't sure it was a no.

"No?" This was not part of the Greatest Idea. The police were supposed to be right behind them. Now the police weren't *coming*?

"For pizza sake, why *not*?"

For a few strides, Vee didn't reply. Then she said through clenched teeth, "Because I didn't want to touch the ATP with goose-poo hands!"

Sunny desperately wanted to laugh, but she couldn't and run and breathe at the same time. Besides, Vee's face made it quite clear it would not be appreciated.

Pounding hooves sounded behind the girls and Major the mini galloped past them, tossing his head and prancing. The Shirt turned and yelled, "Get that horse away from me. He's crazy."

Then he fell smack into a chuckhole, similar to the one that Sunny already had.

Five steps later, the Squad gathered around him. Major the mini, done prancing, breathed his warm breath on Sunny's shoulder blade. He bumped her. Hard.

"Ow, Major, that hurt."

He bumped her again, and she fell on the creepy carnival guy. *Way too close to him.*

He shoved at her, tried to get up, and fell back.

Sunny scrambled to her feet and took a wary step away from Major. "Do you need a time-out?" she asked, brushing off her capris and feeling the bulge of the velvet bag in her pant leg pocket. Major knocked her hand against the bag.

Tilting her head, she glared at the mini, who was once again ducking his head and butting her with increasing intensity. His head against that pocket in her pants.

"Is this a Great—whoa, Major!"

Another—major—bump and Sunny sprawled on the bad guy. This time she rolled off slowly.

Bob chewed his cud as he watched the guy yell about his foot and stupid girls then bleated, "Bahhhhhb!"

The Shirt's eyes bulged. He craned his neck around. "That was a *goat* not a *ghost?*"

Which Way flapped over to the man and hissed, sticking his neck out. The man shrank back, his face turning pale in the moonlight. "What a great idea *this* was supposed to be," he snarled, flopping his head back and holding his ankle up. "Just what do you think you four puny girls are going to do to me?"

"You shouldn't have been mean to the animals," Aneta said, advancing on him, holding up something that made The Shirt drop his foot on the ground to get away and then howl in pain. Her face was stern in the moonlight.

"You shouldn't have called me fat," Esther said, coming alongside the blond. "I have a weapon, and I'm not afraid to use it."

The man used words the girls were *never* allowed to use.

Vee stuck her weapon up close under his chin. "You shouldn't have made me fall in goose poo."

Could the normally gentle S.A.V.E. Squad become a mob like in Uncle Dave's movies and finish off The Shirt? He had been so mean. He had stolen. Nobody would blame them.

Sunny smacked him on his chest as he struggled to rise. "I'm armed, too. The police are coming." *I hope.* "You shouldn't have called me stupid."

The girls moved in. The Shirt's eyes widened in terror.

Sirens whined faintly then gathered volume.

Chapter 27

A Major Idea

Sheriff Bucholtz pursed his lips as he surveyed The Shirt on the ground. A slight tug at the corner of his mouth broke the stern lines of his face. The four S.A.V.E. Squad members stood in a straight line like soldiers. The zoo did not. Major wuffled in Sunny's ear.

"Stop that," she said out of the corner of her mouth.

"So," the sheriff said finally, looking up at the crowd gathered in the moonlit meadow. "Sorry we were late, but it appears you girls have everything under control."

The girls learned Esther hollering, *"You better stop. We're armed and dangerous"* had awakened Uncle Dave. A quick look out his bedroom window, and he was on the phone with the sheriff. Then he'd called all the parents. Vee's mom was there with Bill, whose shoulders kept shaking like it was cold out, but it wasn't.

Aneta's mom was there. She hadn't been home too long coming from the ranch when Uncle Dave called her. Esther's dad was there; her mom was home with the brothers. And Sunny's parents and her brothers. "So," the sheriff repeated, "why was it necessary to truss him up like a turkey?"

He pointed to The Shirt, wrapped neatly from neck to toes in a very old, very long, dirty rope. Aneta and Esther stepped forward.

"That was us, sir." Esther gestured to Aneta who had on her serious face then pointed at herself. "He called me fat."

"He was mean to the zoo," Aneta added, her ponytail bobbing with each emphatic word.

"Of course." Sheriff Bucholtz waved a hand at the three creatures doing what they did when they had nothing else to do. Chewing, flapping, whiffling. "This, I take it, is the zoo?"

"Yep." Sunny gestured toward the house. "Which Way is the goose. Piggles is back there—"

"We encountered him," the sheriff interrupted.

"The pygmy goat is Bob—"

The sheriff nodded as though being introduced to a zoo were an everyday occurrence. "And the broken bottom of a fan rake propped against the guy's face?"

"A lousy goat. It was just a lousy *goat!*" The Shirt moaned, his voice muffled.

Sunny raised her hand. "That was me. He called me a stupid kid. Besides, he was using"—she glanced at her brothers and lowered her voice just like her mom did when her brothers had messed up big-time—"inappropriate words. The rake shut him up. Especially when Which Way sat on it."

"Oh, Sunny," her mother murmured, wiping her eyes and coughing. "You are too much."

The Shirt rolled so the rake fell off his face. "Get me up. You got nothing on me more than trespassing. Stupid girls." He began the rumbling evil laugh, but stopped abruptly as Vee's weapon slid close to his throat.

"That brings us to the rusty pair of spurs ready to slit his throat?"

the sheriff asked mildly.

Vee stepped close to The Shirt. "He"—she jabbed the green-stained finger in his direction—"made me fall in *goose poo!*"

A collective "Ewww" rose from the audience. Sunny looked at her parents and sniffed in Vee's direction. "Yeah, it's bad."

Sunny's dad and Sheriff Bucholtz unrolled The Shirt from the rope. While the sheriff put the cuffs on him, The Shirt threw his shoulders back. "You got me on trespassing. That's it." Puffing out his chest, he said, "Go on. Search me. I should sue."

Sunny folded her arms across her chest.

Said nothing.

Made her smile stay on the inside.

Vee, Esther, and Aneta, however, stiffened then surrounded Sunny and dragged her off to the side.

"He doesn't—," began Vee.

"Your pocket—" Esther was in a panic.

"Our Greatest Idea—" Aneta's eyes brimmed with tears that sparkled in the moonlight.

"Watch," was all Sunny said.

By now Sunny's mom had taken the brothers back to the ranch to avoid The Shirt's continuing vocabulary. Sunny wished she had a handful of goose poo.

When the sheriff got to the cargo pocket on the man's pants, he patted the pocket, unzipped it, and drew out a soft black velvet bag.

"The jewels!" Vee, Aneta, and Esther's voices squeaked together. They whipped around to spear Sunny with the stink eye.

The Shirt's mouth gaped. Then his gaze transferred to Sunny.

"I told you I wasn't stupid," she said.

Chapter 28

Sunny Finishes

I finished!" Sunny placed the manure scraper inside the tool closet in the barn, removed her gloves, and spun. "Yayness!"

Chores were *finished*, chili she'd made was *finished* in a humongous Crock-Pot borrowed from Esther's church, and—she heard high, excited voices of the Squad spilling from the vehicles pulling into the driveway—guests were *finished* coming.

Yes, Sunny Quinlan, *you've got this finishing stuff down.*

"Hey, Sunny girl!" Uncle Dave hollered from the porch, waving a crutch. "Is that frozen pie in the box supposed to be on the counter in the bathroom?"

For pizza sake: *almost* down.

Vee, Esther, and Aneta rushed into the barn; they did a group dance, arms around shoulders, sidestepping. "The Squad did it again!" Esther said, breathless.

"C'mon, guys, let's eat before my brothers get all the corn bread. I'm starving." Sunny led the way into the house. "It's time to celebrate finishing!"

"You made *corn bread*?" Esther sounded impressed.

Sunny shook her head no. Some things were better to *not* start.

The girls had promised each other they wouldn't reveal any more of the deets to their families until this group supper. Now that everyone was seated around the long kitchen table with a card table on each end extending the space so everyone had room, the Squad looked at expectant faces.

Esther's family sat across from Bill and Vee's mom. Bill was already entertaining Esther's brothers. Heather and the Twin Terrors were seated next to Sunny's mom who sat with Dad. Vee's dad, *of course*, was out of town. Aneta's mom sat next to Uncle Dave—Vee, Esther, and Sunny were going to watch *that* very closely—and then she and the Squad sat together.

Sheriff Bucholtz in his uniform, as an unexpected guest, sat at the end by Sunny's brothers, whose faces revealed they were *very pleased* about that.

"We're pretty proud of how it all turned out," Sunny's mom said. "Although I won't say I'm glad for all your decisions."

"Some of them are in the *what-were-you-thinking* category," Sunny's dad agreed.

"I'm so sorry that Uncle Dave broke his ankle," Sunny began.

Her uncle stopped her by pounding a crutch on the floor. "Enough with the apologies. It was my idea to have you come out here in the first place. True, I didn't expect *certain* things, like eleven-year-olds buying a zoo, or them capturing a jewel thief, but still—"

The girls swiveled to look at Sunny.

"Wait. *Your* idea to come to the ranch? It was *my* Great Idea!" she said, leaning forward so she could see him.

"Sorry, Sunny girl. When your dad called to ask me if I would mind—"

Now she switched her focus to her dad who was trading looks

with her mom. Both of them were stuffing chuckles. "*Dad* called you to see if I—" He'd done it again. Asked her what she thought when he already knew what he was going to do. "*Dad!*"

Uncle Dave leaned back in his chair. "Yeah, I thought it would be great for you to come work at the ranch. We're a lot alike. We both like stuff to be fun."

"Tell her your nickname growing up," Sunny's mom said.

Uncle Dave belted out one of his rat-a-tat laughs. "Sisters never forget. It was Halfway Dave. I finished everything halfway, which—"

"—isn't finished at all." This reminded Sunny of the Adventure Readers and Major. "Hey, I'd like to finish something else,"—she placed heavy emphasis on her next words—"besides catching a jewel thief, taking care of Crutch Man, a secondhand zoo, and an entire ranch"—she swept out an arm to include the Squad who were enjoying this family exchange very much—"with the rocko-socko help of the S.A.V.E. Squad."

"What's that?" Esther asked.

"I want to finish the Adventure Readers to the end of the year with Major visiting them at the library to read with them."

"Me, too!" Aneta said. "I cannot wait!"

"But, Sunny." Vee's face lost all its amusement. "We have to adopt out the zoo. *Major isn't staying here.*"

The room dropped into an unnatural silence. Even the brothers stopped chewing.

She'd completely forgotten about finishing with the zoo. They seemed like so much a part of the ranch. . . .

Ughness.

Some celebration.

Now all eyes were on Uncle Dave, who shifted in his seat. He cleared his throat. "Well, Sunny, you know I came here to set up a sport pony breeding stable."

"I know," Sunny said miserably. "You kept telling me." Her heart hurt. No more wuffling in her ear. No more schoolwork buddy. Her brothers might tease her, but it was highly likely she was going to bust out crying and run out of the room.

Esther and Vee had both narrowed their eyes and said together, "And?"

"I'm taking a step back from that. Instead I'm going to create a search and rescue training center with secondhand horses. I've been on the phone a lot with some buddies of mine—"

"You mean all those phone calls weren't about sport ponies?" Sunny slit her eyes at her uncle, who was grinning hugely. "Why didn't you tell me?"

"Oh, because I figured you could practice arguing with me and not get in trouble with your parents. So you can rest easy. The zoo has a home here." He leaned back in his chair. "Remember the kid with Starbright and his dad out of work?"

Vee said, "Oh yes."

Esther snickered.

Vee dealt her the Vee Stare.

"Well, he's a construction builder kind of guy as well as a horseman. I'm going to hire him to build what we need and take care of the horses as they come in. Police departments and border patrol are using horses more and more. Horses are quite sensitive to what's happening around them."

Sunny choked on her corn bread. "They sure are."

The sheriff stood up. Sunny had forgotten he was there.

"I've enjoyed this dinner, but it's time for me to head out." He looked at the girls. "Dave asked me to come and answer any questions you might have since yesterday."

"What's the story?" Esther asked. "Where did he steal the jewels from? Why did he decide to hide them here?"

The sheriff jammed his hands into his utility belt. "That creepy carnival guy, as you girls call him, is Evan Wangston. He and his partners broke into a pretty big jewelry store in Seattle. Wangston dreamed up this idea that he would bring the jewels to Canada with this traveling carnival coming through Oregon. Nobody would think to look for him there and nobody would suspect that millions of dollars—"

A sharp intake of breath from each person at the table. The Squad gulped.

Sunny recalled The Shirt's panic over Bob. She asked, "Why was the guy so freaked out about Bob the goat? I mean, he's just a little goat."

The sheriff laughed deep in his throat. "During the heist, Wangston got scared and shot a night guard who had woken up just as they were departing with the loot. Wangston was sure he'd killed him. His guilty conscience thought the guard's ghost was haunting him. Wangston's not the sharpest tack in the box." Sheriff Bucholtz rocked back on his heels. "The guard's name is *Bob*, and he's not dead."

Vee had the next question, and everyone learned that Wangston had conceived the idea to double-cross his buddies and disappear when the girls offered to buy the zoo. He planned to give the gang the slip and stash the gems at the ranch. Then when he was sure his gang didn't know where he was, he'd circle back and collect the bag. Except his great idea had collided with Sunny's mission to regain her family's trust in finishing things.

"His great idea," Sunny murmured.

Raising a crutch instead of his hand, Uncle Dave asked, "I've got a question. Why would the guy be so stupid to say he didn't have the jewels when he had to know you were going to search him?"

"That is something we just can't figure out," the sheriff said. "It was a pretty stupid bluff."

"Some criminals are stupid. Eleven-year-olds are not," Sunny said, her heart light again, lighter than the moon and shining as brightly. Major was staying. Piggles, Which Way, and Bob would help other kids learn to read on ranch visits. Major the reading mini. Major, who knew when to have a Great Idea at *just the right time.* Evan Wangston knew that.

Complete yayness.

Uncle Dave reached under the table and brought out a small paper bag. "Just to show you there's no hard feelings about you girls and my accident and recovery. . ."

He dug into the bag and handed four jewelry boxes to Aneta's mom. "Could you deliver? I'm not sure I could get around the table without clubbing someone."

Ms. Jasper popped up and handed the boxes around. Once each girl had her box, they shut their eyes and said, "Okay, on three. One-two-three!"

Sunny opened her eyes. In her palm was a glass bead in the shape of a horseshoe fixed to a small, gleaming piece of wood. There were red, green, and crystal sparkle dots curving around it. A tiny silver loop hung at the top.

"Beautiful, and these are the jewels!" Aneta untied her bracelet.

The other girls followed and added the bead, knotting the soft leather cord before and after the bead as they had the others. Then they put their wrists together. "The S.A.V.E. Squad! Together!"

Vee was having some trouble with timing. "Mr. Martin, it was only yesterday that we caught the bad guy. How did you get these so fast?"

Uncle Dave tipped his head toward Aneta's mom who had returned to her chair. "FedEx and knowing a woman who has family members who know everybody everywhere."

"Are the jewels real?" Esther wanted to know, holding up her arm to see the bead twinkle in the overhead light.

"No," Uncle Dave said with a grin and then jerked a thumb toward the sheriff.

The sheriff headed for the door with a slight wave. "No real gems on that bead, girls," and then with a wink at Uncle Dave, who covered his ears, "but the insurance reward money for the recovery of the rubies, emeralds, and diamonds is *very real.*"

"Yes!" the Squad shrieked—loudly.

But then, so did everyone else.

Shirley the palomino was enjoying Esther's attention while Mondo stood just far enough from the railing so no one could touch him. Major, Mystery, and Bob were playing animal soccer with the giant ball. Starbright wiggled himself in between Shirley and Mondo so he wouldn't miss any nose scratches. The girls were on their own with Uncle Dave at the ranch for the rest of the weekend.

"The Squad was amazing," Sunny said reflectively. She couldn't stop smiling and had only ceased spinning when her dinner felt threatened. She clambered up next to Vee.

"I want us to always be together," Esther agreed. "I would hate it if we weren't the Squad anymore."

"I love us," Aneta said inside the corral so she could better watch the soccer game.

"What? Yes, we're the best squad on the planet." Vee obviously was worrying about something. "I still don't get it." She hunkered on the top railing, her brow furrowed, absently braiding Starbright's mane. "You had the bag in your pocket. Then it *wasn't* in your pocket. It was in *Wangston's* pocket."

In the corral, Major picked up a hoof and placed it on the ball, rolling it back and forth. He looked straight at Sunny, lowered his head, and butted the ball toward her. Hard. Then stomped his foot as though to say, "Go ahead, tell 'em!"

"Let's just say, it was a secondhand mini being Major with a bumping nose." Sunny hugged her arms around herself, smiling at the miniature horse. Oh yes.

She loved being a Squader.

And she loved a *Great Idea.*

Lauraine Snelling is an award-winning author with more than seventy-five published titles including two horse-themed series for kids. With more than three million books in print, Lauraine still finds time to create great stories as she travels around the country to meet readers with her husband and rescued basset Winston.

When **Kathleen Wright**'s not dreaming up adventures for her characters, she's riding bikes with her husband, playing pickleball, and trying to convince her rescued border collie that Mom knows best. She taught writing to fifth graders and up and loves how kids think.

Since they can't save the whole world, what about a small piece of it? Four sixth-grade girls join together as The S.A.V.E. Squad and set out to rescue homeless dogs, Dumpster cats, secondhand horses, and owls.

Get your parents' permission and go to The S.A.V.E. Squad's website to check out a quiz and read all about kids and pets! www.TheSAVESquad.com

Catch Up on The S.A.V.E. Squad Adventures with Books 1 & 2

Dog Daze

ISBN 978-1-61626-560-1

The Great Cat Caper

ISBN 978-1-61626-566-3

Available wherever books are sold